WHO LET THE DOG OUT?

ALSO BY DAVID ROSENFELT

ANDY CARPENTER NOVELS

Hounded

Unleashed

Leader of the Pack

One Dog Night

Dog Tags

New Tricks

Play Dead

Dead Center

Sudden Death

Bury the Lead

First Degree

Open and Shut

THRILLERS

Without Warning

Airtight

Heart of a Killer

On Borrowed Time

Down to the Wire

Don't Tell a Soul

NONFICTION

Lessons from Tara: Life Advice from the World's Most Brilliant Dog

Dogtripping: 25 Rescues, 11 Volunteers, and 3 RVs on Our Canine Cross-Country Adventure

WHO LET THE DOG OUT?

David Rosenfelt

MINOTAUR BOOKS

NEW YORK

WHO LET THE DOG OUT? Copyright © 2015 by Tara Productions, Inc. All rights reserved. Printed in the United States of America. For information, address St. Martin's Press, 175 Fifth Avenue, New York, N.Y. 10010.

www.minotaurbooks.com

The Library of Congress Cataloging-in-Publication Data is available upon request.

ISBN 978-1-250-05533-0 (hardcover)
ISBN 978-1-4668-5991-3 (e-book)

Minotaur books may be purchased for educational, business, or promotional use. For information on bulk purchases, please contact the Macmillan Corporate and Premium Sales Department at 1-800-221-7945, extension 5442, or write to specialmarkets@macmillan.com.

First Edition: July 2015

10 9 8 7 6 5 4 3 2 1

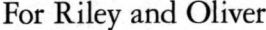

For Riley and Oliver

WHO LET THE DOG OUT?

This was not going to take a master thief. The difficulty of robberies, Gerry Downey knew, was directly proportional to the fear and expectation that the targets had of being robbed. No one goes to extremes to protect property unless they think someone might want to take that property. That's why banks and jewelry stores are tougher targets than hot dog stands and city dumps.

It's Robbery 101.

That was why Downey, who over time had accumulated enough real-world robbery credits to earn his master's, had no concerns about his current job. But that did not mean he was careless about it. He was a pro, and knew it was the easy ones that could occasionally throw you a curve. Which is why he had staked this one out for three days. After all, he was a professional and would act like one, despite the demeaning nature of this particular job.

Of course, the job wasn't just demeaning; it was also strange. Downey had never stolen anything like this before, and likely never would again. But if the payoff was always going to be this good, he'd happily sign on for a repeat performance anytime.

The building was on Route 20 in Paterson, New Jersey, a

heavily trafficked road that had a number of commercial busi-
nesses on it. Part of that time he had been watching from a
hamburger place across the road, which turned out to be bearable
because the burgers were charcoal broiled and damn good and
the French fries were crisp.

The guy who ran the place he was watching, Willie Miller,
left with his wife most days at around five o'clock in the evening, sometimes a little later. The exact timing seemed to
depend on whether they were there alone, or whether a customer
was on site. But so far neither Willie nor anyone else had come
back once they left, and Downey had watched until eight o'clock
each night.

Downey had gone inside the target building the previous
morning, pretending to be a customer himself. He needed to
learn whether there was a burglar alarm (there was) and whether
there were indoor cameras (there were). Neither would cause him
any concern.

On this day Miller and his wife didn't leave until five-fifteen,
so Downey waited twenty minutes and then drove over. There
was no reason not to do it in daylight. If for any reason anyone was
watching, a car pulling up to that building would seem more
natural then than at night. And besides, he would only be there a
few minutes.

Downey picked the lock in less than ten seconds, and went
inside. He knew the silent alarm would be going off, but he'd
be out long before anyone could respond. He pulled his jacket
up over his head and headed for the electrical box to turn off the
cameras. This was accomplished in a few seconds as well.

The only thing that was annoying Downey at that moment,
other than the indignity of having to do such an easy job, was
the noise. The barking was deafening; he had no idea how Miller
could stand it every day.

Downey went directly to the dog runs, stopping at the fourth one on the right. Inside was a large dog, matching the photo he had been given. He didn't know what kind it was, and didn't care. Dogs didn't interest him one way or the other, and it amazed him how some people talked about them like they were human.

He opened the cage, pulling the leash out of his pocket. The dog seemed friendly enough and not inclined to attack, which was a plus, since if Downey had to shoot her, it would have defeated the purpose of his being there.

But her tail was wagging, and she came over and lowered her head, as if she wanted Downey to pet her. That sure as hell wasn't going to happen, so Downey just put the leash on her and led her out.

Downey took her to his car and she hopped right in. The entire thing hadn't taken more than three minutes, a very profitable three minutes at that.

The man is pure evil. He must be stopped."

"That might be overstating it a bit," Laurie Collins says. "He's a baseball coach, working with nine-year-olds."

I point toward the field. "Do you see where Ricky is? Do you?" I'm talking about our recently adopted son, currently positioned in the outfield.

"Of course I do. He's in right field."

I nod vigorously. "Exactly! Right field! That's where they put the losers, the guys they're trying to hide. Nobody good plays right field."

"Ruth, Aaron, Kaline, Clemente, Frank Robinson, Andre Dawson . . ." The only team sport that Laurie likes is baseball; she loves the history and tradition, and she's a student of it. If I don't interrupt, she'll name fifty great right fielders.

"Believe me, those guys didn't play right field in Little League," I say. "They pitched or played shortstop. In the majors, right field is fine; in Little League it's Death Valley. This coach has no idea what he's doing."

"Don't talk to him, Andy. Don't be one of those parents."

The coach is Bill Silver, and since he's at least six-two and 210

5

pounds, there's no way that I, Andy Carpenter, am going to confront him. I can't be one of "those parents," as Laurie put it, because "those parents" usually aren't cowards.

Laurie and I have been married five months, and we adopted Ricky at the same time. It was too late to get him involved in peewee football, so this is my first chance to see him on an athletic field.

The next batter hits a fly ball to right field. Ricky doesn't panic, just circles under it, waiting patiently for it to come down. And it does in fact come down, about eight feet to the right of where Ricky is standing. Displaying keen baseball instincts, he runs over and picks it up, then throws it to no one in particular, but in the general area of the infield. And it almost reaches the infield by the time it stops rolling.

"Good try, Rick!" Laurie calls out.

"He's a shortstop," I say to no one in particular. "Shortstops don't catch fly balls. You put Derek Jeter out there, and he embarrasses himself. You ever see Cal Ripken try to catch a fly ball? Pathetic."

"Andy, Ricky's having fun."

"You don't get to the majors by having fun," I say.

"Majors?" Laurie says, her voice both incredulous and disapproving. "Is that your plan?"

"Why not? I could have made it to the majors myself, if I had the breaks, and the dedication, and the ability. Why can't Ricky make it?"

"Well, for one thing, maybe he isn't good enough."

"That's because he's not focused on baseball. You need to stop bothering him, cluttering his head with that other stuff."

"What other stuff?"

"You know . . . like reading and math. When is he going to

need that junk in his life? Nobody reads anymore; everything is video."

"Andy . . ." I've got a hunch that the next words out of Laurie's mouth are not going to be "I agree with you completely." But I don't get to hear them, because my cell phone rings and she stops in midsentence.

Caller ID tells me that it's Willie Miller, my former client and current partner in the Tara Foundation, our dog rescue operation. Willie and his wife, Sondra, are completely dedicated to finding loving homes for the dogs we bring in.

"What's up?" is the way I answer the phone.

"We've had a robbery," he says.

"At your house?"

"No, at the foundation. Sondra and I went to get something to eat after work, and when we got home I noticed that the alarm had gone off. So I came down here to see what was going on. There was a break-in."

I'm a little confused, because there is really nothing to steal there. We don't keep money or valuables in that building, just dogs. "What did they steal?"

"The shepherd mix. Cheyenne."

"I'll be right there," I say to Willie, and then turn to Laurie, who has overheard my end of the conversation. "Somebody stole a dog from the foundation."

"That's bizarre," she says, which is true. These are dogs up for adoption; there should be no reason for someone to steal one. "You go down there; I'll get a ride home with Sally."

Sally Rubenstein is our neighbor, and her son Will is on the same team as Ricky. They are best friends, but unfortunately, Will is playing shortstop, and he fields grounders like Ozzie Smith.

"Okay. If you get a chance after the game, talk to Coach Silver about Ricky."

"What do you want me to say?" she asks.

"Tell him Ricky should play in the infield or pitch. Don't overtly threaten him, but make sure he sees your gun." Laurie is an ex-cop and the private investigator for my law practice, and she carries a handgun.

"Good-bye, Andy."

T he guy shut the cameras off. And he picked the lock. He knew what he was doing."

I have to agree with Willie on his assessment, though it seems to make very little sense. Why would an accomplished thief come in and take a stray dog that was already up for adoption?

"You look at the tape?" I ask. "We get anything before he shut it off?" The cameras were not designed to capture thieves in action; we never contemplated that there might be a need. They were actually set up as a webcam, so Willie can see from his home what's going on with the dogs, in case any are sick. Cheyenne's run would therefore be within view of one of the cameras.

"Nah. He had his head covered with his sweatshirt; from some kind of college, I think. But we've got the GPS, unless the guy removed it."

They make inexpensive GPS devices that are small and attach to dogs' collars. We started using them about six months ago, when one of the dogs we adopted out escaped from his new owner. We searched for three days before we found the poor dog. If a dog is going to get away, it is likely to be before he or she is acclimated to the new home, so now we do the GPS thing as a service to protect both the dog and the adopter.

"Let's take a look."

We go into the office, and Willie takes the tracking machine out of the cabinet. He turns it on, and we wait the few seconds until it's ready. Once it is, Willie punches in the number that identifies Cheyenne's collar.

"We got it," he says. "Twenty-sixth Street, off Nineteenth Ave. Let's go."

"We should call the police," I say. "Have them meet us there."

"The police? For a stray dog? We can handle this."

Willie is a black belt in karate and one of the toughest people I've ever met. He can also be very nice, as evidenced by the fact that he used the pronoun "we." He knows very well that if there is any "handling" to be done, I'll be of little use.

"I'm not saying we can't handle it, but—"

"Andy, if he takes the GPS collar off and then leaves with the dog, we could lose him. Let's go; you can call the cops on the way if you want."

We head for my car, and I call Pete Stanton as we drive. Pete is a Paterson Police captain, and a very good friend of mine. I reach him on his cell and tell him what's going on.

"So what do you want from me?" he asks.

"To meet us there, arrest the bad guy, do your job, protect the public. That kind of thing."

"Willie can handle it," he points out.

"That's what I'm afraid of." Willie has been known to be somewhat protective of our dogs. If this guy has hurt Cheyenne, Willie might impose the death penalty on him. "What else have you got to do?"

"Not much; I'm just trying to apprehend a murderer."

There was a local murder last week, and the suspected perpetrator, Eric Brantley, has eluded capture despite an all-out man-hunt. He is accused of killing his business partner with a well-placed bullet in the back of the head.

"The only way you're going to catch him is if he comes in voluntarily and surrenders," I say. "And even then you'll probably screw it up. Come on, this won't take more than twenty minutes."

"You're a pain in the ass, you know?" Pete asks.

"I am aware of that." I'm also aware that Pete could never turn me down for anything, since it was just a few months ago that I successfully defended him when he was wrongly accused of murder. I am ridiculously wealthy, mostly through inheritance, so I didn't charge him for the defense. Therefore he will owe me until the end of time, and I intend to take advantage of it for even longer than that.

I give him the address, and he agrees to meet us there. We're going to get there before him, but we can decide how to handle things when we arrive.

The house the GPS leads us to is modest and a little run-down, but no more so than the others in the neighborhood. This is not a wealthy area; most of the residents are honest, hardworking people who struggle to make ends meet. I never thought of them as a particularly dog-thieving group.

There is still daylight left, so the fact that there seem to be no lights on in the house is not particularly significant. Nor is the fact that there is no car in the driveway; there are plenty of cars parked on the street, and one of them could be the car that brought Cheyenne here.

We park and get out of the car. Willie starts toward the front porch of the house, showing no hesitation whatsoever.

"Let's wait for Pete," I say.

"We don't need Pete."

"I'm sure that's true, but there's no downside to waiting. He'll be here in five minutes, and it's not like they can leave without us seeing them."

"Come on, Andy. I want a shot at this guy. He won't tell the cops why he did it."

"He won't tell us either."

"Oh, yes he will," Willie says, and I believe him.

But I convince him to wait, and my job is made easier by the fact that Pete pulls up within two minutes. He gets out of the car, and we update him on the little that has happened so far.

Pete frowns at the indignity of having to deal with this as he starts up the steps. Willie is right up alongside him, and I'm a couple of paces back. I'd just as soon wait in the car, or even better, at home, but I'm actually not that afraid. Unless there's a Russian battalion setting up an ambush in that house, Pete and Willie can handle this.

Pete rings the bell, and immediately a dog starts barking.

"That's Cheyenne," Willie says, immediately.

"How do you know that?" Pete asks.

"I recognize the bark," Willie says, but I think he's lying. There's nothing about the bark that is distinctive, and we've only had Cheyenne for a few days. Besides, when one dog barks at the foundation, they all do, so I doubt he's ever heard Cheyenne's bark when it wasn't drowned out by all the others.

The barking stops, but no one comes to the door. Pete rings the bell again, which restarts the barking, but once again fails to turn up any humans.

"Nobody here," Pete says.

"Cheyenne's here," Willie points out. "Let's go in and get her."

"You've got probable cause for a robbery," I point out to Pete. "The stolen merchandise is barking."

He turns to Willie. "How do you know it's your dog?"

"Because it's MY dog. So I know her bark."

Pete rings the bell again, with the now predictable result . . . more barking, but that's it. After a few moments, he takes out his gun, which I assume is proper procedure when entering a crime scene in this fashion.

He reaches for the door handle, and seems surprised to find that it turns and the door opens. "Wait here," he says, which I am quite happy to do.

Willie is less inclined to follow the order, and when Pete enters the house, Willie is right behind him, leaving me alone on the porch. Alone is not my favorite state of being in situations like this, so I belatedly join the procession.

There is a staircase directly across from the door, off the foyer, and since I'm a few seconds late, I don't know whether Pete and Willie went into the room to the left of the staircase or the room to the right. I'm about to call out to them when I hear a bark, which is clearly to the left. So that's where I go.

Huge mistake.

Cheyenne stops barking when she sees me. She is sitting on the floor about five feet from a recliner chair in what probably passes as the den, with a leash still around her neck. The room has a sofa, a table with a small TV resting on it, and the chair.

In the chair is a dead body. As a criminal attorney, I have seen way more than my share of them, both in photographs and sometimes in person. While I don't make it a practice to rank them, it's safe to say that this is not one I am soon going to forget.

The victim looks to be in his forties, well built, dressed in jeans and a Syracuse University sweatshirt. My guess would be that he's about six feet tall, but it's hard to tell because he's sitting down, and mostly decapitated. His throat has been sliced, and his head hangs to the side, only partially connected to his torso. His hands are behind him, probably tied behind the chair, but I'm not about to go back there to find out.

No one is going to have to feel for a pulse to know that this guy is history, and establishing time of death is not going to be a problem, because before I turn away I think I can see that the blood is still flowing.

It's hard for me to accurately take in the scene, because I'm trying to do it while gagging, screaming, and running out of the room. As I'm leaving, Pete and Willie have heard me and are running in. They're going to understand my reaction soon enough; there's no reason for me to stop and explain it to them.

I run out on the porch and try to take deep breaths and avoid throwing up. I haven't thrown up since I was a kid, and just the memory of how awful it was makes me want to throw up. I can hear Pete yelling something inside the house, but I can't tell what it is.

Moments later, Willie comes out with Cheyenne on the leash, and he hands it to me. "Keep an eye on her," he says, and when I take the leash he goes back into the house.

So I'm left on the porch, simultaneously retching, gasping, panicking, and holding a leash. Fortunately, I'm a multitasker.

It's less than five minutes before the police cars start to arrive, and there must be ten of them. Pete comes out to talk to two of the officers. Pete is a captain in robbery/homicide, so I assume he's in charge, and just consulting.

He hasn't said anything to me since we discovered the body, but when he sees me still on the porch, he comes over. "You and the dog should wait over there," he says. "You're going to need to give a statement."

"You know everything I know."

He nods. "We have to get it all on paper." Then he points to Cheyenne. "Too bad he can't talk."

"She."

"What?"

"She's a female. Her name is Cheyenne."

"Thanks," he says, with a slight frown. "That's just the kind of information we need."

"What's the victim's name?" I ask.

"According to his driver's license, Gerald Downey. You know him?"

I don't, and I tell him so. Then, "Any evidence of a break-in?"

Pete frowns again. "You conducting a formal investigation? Or maybe looking for a client?"

"No chance. My last client was such a pain in the ass, I'm retired." Since Pete was my last client, the dig isn't that subtle.

"The back door was open; that could have been the point of entry, and it's possible the perpetrator took off that way when we showed up. The wound was very fresh."

"I noticed," I say. "And after our statements, we can take Cheyenne back to the foundation?"

He nods. "Yeah. I don't see her as a suspect. Maybe you can represent her in a civil suit."

Crime scenes take forever to process, and when the crime is murder, then "forever" understates the case. It's almost three hours before Willie and I give our statements and are cleared to leave.

Willie has Cheyenne's leash, and he comes over and says, "I'm going to take her home with me, just in case."

"Okay."

"You get a look at the guy's face?" he asks.

"Not really. . . . Once I saw it wasn't attached to his neck, I didn't really focus on it."

"I did; he came in yesterday. Said he was interested in adopting a dog."

"Which one? Cheyenne?"

Willie shrugs. "I don't know; it never got that far. I asked him where the dog would sleep, and he said he had a doghouse, so I got rid of him."

"He was probably just checking the place out," I say.

Willie and Cheyenne leave, and before I go I find Pete and ask him if he's learned any more about the victim.

"Did I say anything to give you the impression that you and I were conducting a joint investigation?" he asks.

"A guy steals my dog and then gets murdered; I can't help but wonder if the two are somehow connected."

"Your dog wasn't the only thing this guy stole."

"He had a record?"

He nods. "That's understating it. Been a thief his whole life, spent a bunch of it doing time. Hasn't been arrested in the last two years, which is a record for him."

"What did he steal?"

"Let's put it this way: I think until tonight dogs were the only thing he hadn't stolen. Probably had it on his bucket list before he kicked it." He pauses, then says, "Just got it in under the wire."

There's nothing left to be learned from Pete tonight, so I go home to Laurie, who is awaiting my arrival so eagerly that she has fallen asleep with anticipation.

I take Tara and Sebastian for their nightly walk. Tara is a golden retriever and the greatest dog in the history of the universe. Sebastian is the basset hound we adopted as a package deal along with Ricky. It is poor Sebastian's plight to forever be the second best dog in the house, but he seems to accept it and deals with the humiliation pretty well.

I plan a ten-minute walk, but they appear to enjoy it so much that I extend it to a half hour. When I get back, Laurie has awakened and is sitting up in bed waiting for me.

I had called her from the scene, but now I explain the night's events in more detail. "You think the murder and stealing the dog are connected?" she asks.

I shrug, which is what I do when I don't know something. I find that I shrug a lot. "Beats me."

"You going to look into it?"

"Maybe. I'm curious about it."

Unfortunately, the conversation doesn't get any more insightful than that, and finally she brightens up and starts telling me about the rest of the baseball game. "Ricky hit a home run!"

"He did?"

"Well, I'm not sure it's officially a home run. He hit it about five or six feet toward third base, and then the other team kept throwing the ball away, and he ran all the way around the bases. Then he started going to first again; he thought he could just keep running until they tagged him. It was adorable and he was so excited; I wish you had seen it."

"Aggressive on the bases, and always looking for that extra edge: that's what I like to hear," I say. "I worked with him on that."

"Don't tell him I told you about it," Laurie says. "He wants to tell you himself in the morning."

"Did you talk to the coach about the right field thing?"

She nods. "I did more than talk. I pointed my gun at him and told him either Ricky plays shortstop or the team will be minus one coach."

"Perfect. What did he say?"

"He refused, so I shot him."

"That's my girl."

If you are antisocial, far northern Maine is the place for you. Of course, other preferences and characteristics besides not liking to have people around would help as well. You should be rugged, like living off the land, not care very much about eating out and cable TV, and have a healthy disdain for paved roads.

That's not to say there are no people to be found. There are even a few small towns here and there . . . mostly there. They are nothing much to speak of; in this area three hundred people represents a bustling metropolis.

But the citizens of these towns are for the most part hard-working, self-sufficient, decent people. And those are the kind of people who occupy Fleming, Maine, population 248. Fleming sits about six miles from the Canadian border.

There is another small community, about twelve miles west of Fleming. Populationwise it's far smaller, numbering thirty-one people, a third of whom are Americans. It's not on any map, nor does it have any kind of official government. Its people have only lived there for three weeks, and they have essentially blended into the land, living in caves and camouflaged huts. They don't have to farm the land: they have their own supplies, enough to last them for another three months.

That is much more than they will need; they will very likely all be dead well before that.

The citizens of Fleming have no idea that this community exists. The people almost never come into town, or make their presence known. They have sent in two of their group, under assumed names and false identities, to get something they hadn't anticipated needing.

Before long, when they get the word, they will break into units of two and three and travel south. They will take back roads, which is pretty much the only available roads anyway.

They will head to a small town called Ashby, which is actually an island, connected to the mainland by a small bridge. There are 740 people in Ashby at this time of year, far more than in the winter.

The people of Ashby are not expecting these visitors, and their town was chosen for no reason other than unlucky geography. It is situated perfectly: if there were a bull's-eye, Ashby would be in the center of it. The citizens of Ashby will not even realize the invaders are there until it is too late.

By that point their fate will have been sealed.

Coincidences bug me. They don't bug me as much as people who wait until all their groceries are rung up before reaching for their wallet or opening their purse. And they don't bug me nearly as much as drivers I wave ahead of me, who then neglect to thank me. Or as much as football announcers who refer to simple blocking as putting "a hat on a hat," or who say that the solution to a team's problem is the need to have someone "step up and make a play." And coincidences don't bug me anywhere close to as much as DVD packages that can only be opened with a chain saw.

But they do bug me, and I basically don't believe in them.

As coincidences go, this would be a pretty big one. Literally minutes after entering our foundation building, going directly to Cheyenne's run, and stealing Cheyenne, Gerald Downey was brutally murdered.

Very little of it makes sense, at least at the moment. If Cheyenne was Downey's dog, and she got lost, then why go through the elaborate theft? He could have simply showed up at the foundation and provided evidence of ownership, and we would have turned her over.

That evidence would have been easy to provide, be it vet

records or even a photograph. Everyone has some photographs of their dog, even slimeballs like Downey. We have no interest in making it difficult for owners; we want them to reunite with their dogs.

If Downey did not own Cheyenne, then why steal her? She's a great dog, but there are thousands of great dogs available in area shelters and with rescue groups. She's a mutt, so she would have no value if he was looking to sell her.

Maybe Downey was stealing her for someone else, and for some reason that other person couldn't or wouldn't come down to the foundation and identify her as his dog. Might that person have killed Downey? But if he did, why not take Cheyenne? If she was important enough to hire Downey to steal her, why leave her there?

As I may have mentioned, these are the kind of questions that bug me.

I want to talk to Laurie about it some more, but I can't do it at breakfast. Since Ricky has joined our family, we try and eat as many meals together as possible. Occasionally our schedules prevent us from all being home for dinner, but when it comes to breakfast, we're pretty much at one hundred percent.

Laurie, overprotective mother that she is, doesn't want to discuss things like murder and near decapitations in front of Ricky. But Ricky fills the conversational space; he's in a very talkative mood this morning.

"I hit the ball yesterday."

"Yeah, I'm sorry I missed it. I heard it was a home run."

"Mom tell you that?"

"She did. She's very proud of you."

"I just hit it a little bit, and then the other team made a lot of errors." He turns to Laurie. "That's not a home run, Mom." He gives me a little eye roll, a gesture that seems to say that we guys should know better than to believe women when it comes to something like baseball.

"I thought it was great," Laurie says.

Laurie and I basically take turns walking Ricky to and from school. He goes to School Number 20, which is about a fifteen-minute walk from our house. It's where I went to school, and it looks absolutely the same.

When it's my turn, as it is today, I often take Tara and Sebastian with us, which becomes their second walk of the morning. But Laurie says she'd like to come along today, and suggests we leave the dogs at home. It seems like a strange request, but I wait until we've dropped Ricky off to ask what's going on.

"I know you want to talk some more about what happened last night. Coincidences bug you, and you want to look into it."

"How did you know that?"

"You're not exactly inscrutable, Andy."

"I need to work on that."

She holds up a set of car keys. "Let's go," she says, and we walk back to our car and head over to the murder scene.

If you ever want to attract a crowd, wrap yourself in police tape. Long after a criminal event has occurred, people seem drawn to the scene by the presence of that tape, as an apparent signal that "excitement occurred here."

But when it comes to bringing out the masses, police tape takes a distant backseat to media trucks, which in turn pale next to reporters and cameramen.

Local news stations have a weird habit of sending those poor people out to the scene of events that have long been over. For example, the other day the Giants signed a free agent running back, and the local sportscaster reported the news at six o'clock in the morning from outside the empty stadium. The reason it was empty is that the season doesn't start for five months, and the running back that was signed was in Milwaukee, where he lives.

But the media people are here at the murder scene, as are heaping helpings of police tape, so crowds are milling about. There are also some cops here, probably wrapping up their investigation, as well as making sure no one enters the house.

Having been a member of the Paterson Police Department, Laurie pretty much knows everyone on it. I know a lot of them also, but since my connection to them has mostly been as a defense attorney attacking them in cross-examination, they have always disliked me rather intensely. I thought my defending Pete, one of their own, might make them think more kindly of me. It hasn't.

So Laurie walks over to talk to a detective named Danny Alvarez, who greets her with a big smile. They talk for a while, and while I can't hear what they're saying, I see Laurie point back toward me. Alvarez looks my way, and loses the smile.

After maybe three minutes, Alvarez walks off the porch and down the driveway, and Laurie comes over to me. I ask her what's going on.

"Alvarez is setting it up for us."

Before I get a chance to ask what that means, Alvarez comes back up the alley and gives Laurie the thumbs-up sign. "Let's go," she says, and I follow her down the same driveway Alvarez had gone down. "We're going to talk to Downey's landlady," she says. "Her name is Helen Streiter."

When we get to the back of the house, I point to the screen door to Downey's house. "Pete said that door was open, that we might have scared the killer off."

We look around at the surroundings. There are houses and driveways everywhere, from both Downey's street and the one behind it. There is not, as I suspected, a doghouse.

"You want to talk to me?" a voice says, and we see that there's a woman waiting at the screen door in the back of the house next door to Downey's. She's wearing something that's either a housecoat or a dress, but whatever it is, she looks like she bought it the year the Cubs won the World Series.

She stands by the open door, with no obvious inclination to let us inside. I can see that she is barefoot, which in context does not seem particularly surprising. "The cop said I was supposed to talk to you, but I ain't got all day," she says with a sneer, immediately getting on my nerves.

"You rushing to get ready for the prom?" I ask.

"What's that supposed to mean?"

Laurie frowns slightly at the unproductiveness of my comment. "Ms. Streiter, we just want to ask you about Gerry Downey's dog," Laurie says.

"Dog? He ain't got no dog. I don't allow no dogs."

"Are you sure about that?"

"Course I'm sure. Anyway, Gerry hated dogs. There's a dog across the street that barks during the night, when he hears noises out on the street. Gerry told me once he was going to shoot the damn thing."

"And it's not possible he could have had a dog without you knowing about it?" I ask.

"A dog that don't bark? That he doesn't have to let out? That nobody knows about? Come on . . . gimme a break."

Gerry Downey didn't own a dog, and didn't like them. Even if those things weren't true, he wouldn't have been allowed to have one where he lived. But he broke into our foundation building and stole one, just before he was brutally murdered.

"He must have stolen Cheyenne for someone else," I say, as we're driving home.

"But not the person that killed him" is Laurie's reply. "Because that person wouldn't have left her there."

"So we need to find out who Downey had been in contact with in the last days before his death," I say.

"We only need to if we really care why Downey stole the dog. You have her back, and Downey is dead. Some people might consider that resolution enough."

I nod. "True. On the other hand, whoever authorized the theft of Cheyenne is still out there, and might do it again. Which would violate our protection philosophy." Willie and I feel that once we rescue a dog it is in our protection, and we have full responsibility for it for the rest of its life, even after we find it a home.

"Why am I not surprised?" Laurie asks.

I respond with a question of my own. "You think we should put Super Sam on it?"

Laurie considers this for a moment. On some recent cases, I have used Sam Willis, my accountant-turned-computer-hacker-extraordinaire, to track movements and contacts of certain subjects of our investigations. He often does this by hacking into phone company records, learning whom the person spoke to. He also can access GPS records and determine where the person's cell phone has been, since each one has a GPS built into it. It's not one hundred percent, but people and their cell phones are rarely in different locations.

"Might as well," she finally says, which serves as evidence that she does not consider what we are doing to be particularly important. Laurie believes in old-fashioned, pavement-pounding police work. She recognizes the value of using technology, but it is rarely her first or preferred option.

Instead of going home, we head down to my office on Van Houten Street. I haven't been there since Pete's trial ended, and if I never go back I'd be fine with it. I'm not exactly a workaholic.

The only reason we're going there now is that Sam's office is down the hall. This way I can talk to Sam, and at the same time drop off a rent check that I forgot to mail. Sofia Hernandez owns the building and operates the fruit stand on the main floor. If I bring her the check in person, she gives me a cantaloupe, and they're always ripe.

My assistant, Edna, is not in, which does not exactly represent a news flash. She's training for a crossword puzzle tournament, and since she hardly ever works even when we have a client, there is no reason at all for her to come in when we don't.

The office is a little dusty. Sofia's daughter, also named Sofia, is supposed to come in and tidy up once a week. I think she may have missed a couple of weeks, but I don't want to get her in trouble by telling her mother. I also don't want to jeopardize my cantaloupe perk.

We're about to head down to Sam's office when he shows up. "I thought I heard you. We have a case?"

Sam considers himself a cross between Sherlock Holmes and Eliot Ness, and closer to the latter. His work as my investigator has soured him on accounting, but that is unfortunately how he makes his living. He wants to be around when the shooting starts, which represents quite a change for him. A few years ago he would have said that Smith & Wesson was an accounting firm in Passaic.

"We don't have a case. We have a research project."

"Oh," he says, obviously disappointed.

"But it involves a murder, and I can't promise, but there's a chance you can shoot someone."

"Cool. Is it the murder on Twenty-sixth Street? The guy who got his neck sliced?"

"That's the one."

"We looking for the slicer?" he asks.

"At this point we just want to learn about the slicee."

"Gerald Downey, right?"

"Right."

Laurie enters the conversation for the first time. "Sam, we think someone hired him to steal something. So we want to know who he's been in contact with the last couple of weeks, and maybe if he received any unusual amounts of money."

"What did he steal?"

"A dog."

"A valuable dog? Like a show dog?" he asks.

"No. A mix."

"That's weird."

"Yes, Sam," I say. "Weird is exactly the word for it."

f you run down to the jail now, you can get
yourself a client," Pete says. Pete knows I have
no interest in a client, so if he's calling me at home to tell me
that someone is in jail, it must relate to the Downey case. "You
made an arrest?"

"I performed extraordinary police work, which resulted in
the perpetrator being brought to justice, and our community
made safer."

"Who is it?"

"Guy's name is Tommy Infante. He's a business associate of
Downey's and they had a dispute. It didn't end well."

"What about Cheyenne?" I ask.

"What does that mean?"

"The dog. Where does she fit in? Was she Infante's dog?"

"Give me a break, Andy. The dog doesn't fit in; it's a dog. The
dispute had nothing to do with the dog. Leave me alone with
the damn dog."

"The victim stole Cheyenne an hour before he got killed.
That's how you found the body in the first place."

"So mention that in the eulogy."

"Do me a favor—"

Pete interrupts. "Another one?"

"It's only just begun. Can you call over to the jail and clear the way for me to see Infante?"

"You're a pain in the ass," Pete says, and hangs up. His gratefulness to me for representing him seems to be wearing off.

I ask Laurie, who has overheard my side of the conversation, "You up for a romantic afternoon at the jail?"

"One of us has to pick up our son at school, unless we get him an apartment there."

I've got a feeling I'm not in line for the father of the year award, because I had completely forgotten about that. I've spent almost forty years trying to learn how to take care of myself, and doing so for another human being does not come naturally.

So I head down to the jail, all by myself, alone and dateless. Laurie's getting overconfident; doesn't she realize that I could pick up the phone and get a hundred women who would jump at the opportunity to go to the jail with me and meet a murderer?

Tommy Infante is in an area of the jail where the accused but not yet convicted are held. It's not as depressing as prison, where hope is pretty much nonexistent. In this pretrial phase there is always the possibility, at least in the accused's mind, that something will happen to derail the process. Maybe the prosecutor will decide there isn't enough evidence to go forward, or they'll arrest somebody else.

The possibility that something great like that could happen is slim, but who knows? It's like if you're a fringe major league player being called into the manager's office. You're hitting 190, so it's likely he's going to tell you he's sending you down to the minors, but there's always a chance he just wants to compliment you on your hustle, or the play you made in the third inning. You've got hope and a chance until you don't have them anymore.

I tell the clerk at the visitor's desk who I am and that I want to see Infante. Pete has done his job and called them, so that part goes smoothly. However, they still have to make sure that Infante is willing to see me, so I sit and wait while that effort is made.

Everything takes forever within the workings of the jail, which makes little sense. By definition, no one has anyplace to go or very much to do, so you'd think they could move a little quicker. I'm very surprised when only twenty minutes have passed before the clerk's phone rings, with the word that Infante will see me.

I'm also surprised when they don't bring me to the visitor's area, where people talk on phones through the glass. Instead I'm led to an anteroom, which must mean they think I am here as Infante's lawyer. I do nothing to dissuade them from thinking this, since I prefer the privacy.

I'm here for five minutes when Tommy Infante is brought in. He's tall, at least six-four, and seems to be in reasonably good shape. He has a clean-cut look about him, and somehow seems out of place in this establishment.

He's in cuffs, and the guard simply points to the empty chair and says, "Sit down." Once Infante does that, the guard unlocks one cuff from his wrist and attaches it to the metal table. He leaves without saying another word.

Infante watches him leave, then turns to me and says, "Quite a talker."

The sarcasm is not world class, but it seems so incongruous to the surroundings that I laugh out loud. Of course, a lawyer laughing in these surroundings is even more incongruous. So we're a couple of fun-loving, walking incongruities.

"You don't seem worried," I say.

"I'm plenty worried. But I'm feeling better that you're here."

"Why?"

"Because I've heard about you. You're a famous lawyer, so you're probably good."

"That's not why I'm here."

"Nobody sent you?" he asks.

It's a strange comment for him to make. "Who would have sent me?"

He shakes his head. "My luck keeps getting worse. Why the hell are you here?"

"Just before Downey was killed, he stole a dog from my rescue foundation."

He looks at me as if I'm nuts. "And?"

"And I was wondering if you knew anything about that. Or maybe if it was your dog."

He thinks for a moment, and then asks, "That's really what this is about?"

I nod. "It is. Sorry if you expected something else."

"Let me ask you a question," he says. "When you have a client in my position, what's the first thing you tell him?"

"Not to say a word to anyone. Talk only to your lawyer."

"Right. And since you just told me you're not my lawyer, why would I possibly want to talk to you, about a dog or anything else?"

It's a good point, and I tell him so. "On the other hand," I say, "I'm trying to figure out what is going on, and I have investigators working on it. There's a chance I can find something out which gets you off the hook."

"Getting off the hook is an appealing idea," he says, and we launch into a mini-negotiation. At its conclusion, he hires me as his lawyer for an hour, and gives me an IOU for one dollar. It binds me to confidentiality regarding anything he might say.

Once that is out of the way, his question is as deflating as it is simple and short.

"Downey stole a dog?"

W hy would he steal a dog?" Tommy presses, his confusion evident.

"That's what I just asked you," I point out, though it's become obvious Tommy is not going to enlighten me on the matter.

"I have no idea," he says. "I never saw Downey with a dog. He wasn't even the dog type."

"How did you know him?"

"We hung out in the same places."

"You were friends?"

He hesitates. "At one point. Not lately."

"Why is that?" I ask.

"We committed a robbery together," he says, and then provides a legally insignificant correction. "He did the robbery; I drove the car."

"What did you steal?'

"We hit a jewelry store in downtown Paterson. I needed the money; I've got a sick kid. Downey never paid me my share."

"So that helps them with motive," I say, more to myself than to him.

"It gets much worse. I ran into Downey in a bar, last Monday night. We had an argument about it, in front of a lot of people."

"Did you threaten him?"

He nods. "I said if he didn't give me my money, I would slit his damn throat."

The first thing they teach you in law school is that when someone gets their throat sliced, it's never good to be the person who threatened to do the slicing. It has a tendency to make the police slightly suspicious.

Infante says that he could never commit such a crime, and certainly didn't do so. He says it was an empty threat, born out of frustration, and he knows how bad that looks.

"Any idea what other evidence they have?" I ask.

He shakes his head. "They couldn't have any, at least nothing legitimate. I didn't do it."

"They wouldn't make the arrest based on just the threat. They have to have something else."

"I didn't kill the guy," he says.

I have no idea if he's telling the truth, and even when I do have instincts in matters like this, I am wrong as often as right. "I'll let you know if I find out anything that you can use."

"I need help," he says. "I need you to help me."

My mind tells my mouth not to answer that, but my mouth rarely cares what my mind says. "I'll take you through the arraignment, and then I'll see to it you get a good lawyer."

I'm not exactly thrilled with the outcome of my meeting with Tommy. I got none of the information that I wanted, and instead wound up with a temporary client that I definitely did not want. It was a lose-lose.

Heading home I find myself starting to accept the fact that I may never find out how or if Cheyenne is tied in to Downey's murder. At this point it would seem the only possible way would be to discover who Cheyenne's previous owner was, but I can't figure out a way to do that.

Cheyenne was found stray, alone on a Paterson street, and was taken to the shelter by an animal control officer. She was held there for the required five days, necessary to give an owner time to find her there. No one claimed her, and soon after that we took her out of the shelter and into our foundation.

I get home just in time for dinner with Laurie and Ricky. We used to order in quite frequently, but since adopting Ricky, Laurie has been cooking a lot more. I think it's some kind of motherly instinct, or something. Whatever it is, I don't think I have it, because tonight I'd rather bring in a pizza.

After dinner, Ricky and I go on our evening walk with Tara and Sebastian. It's time that Tara and I used to have to ourselves, but I find that I enjoy the addition of Ricky and Sebastian. Maybe it's a fatherly instinct.

"Can I talk to you about something, Dad?" Ricky asks. I have to admit, even after these months, I still get a kick out of him calling me Dad.

But I'm also a little worried about the subject of this upcoming talk. Ricky was in his house months ago when his father was gunned down, and it is certainly not unexpected that he's had some difficulties recovering from that trauma. Laurie takes him to see a child therapist twice a week, and while he is by all accounts doing very well, he has his ups and downs.

I don't really know how to handle these kinds of things, and I'm afraid of screwing up, so I try to defer to Laurie whenever possible. This could be one of those times I'm not going to be able to.

"You don't need to ask me that, Rick," I say. "You can always talk to me about anything, at any time."

It turns out that I had completely misjudged the subject matter. "I don't think I want to play baseball anymore" is what he says, and while I am relieved, I am also totally horrified.

"ARE YOU OUT OF YOUR MIND? GIVE UP BASE-
BALL? WHAT ABOUT ME? WHAT ABOUT MY DREAMS?
ARE YOU ONLY THINKING ABOUT YOURSELF?" I don't
actually say any of these things; I'm way too mature for that.

"How come, Rick?" is what I actually say.

"It's not so much fun."

My heart is heavy. It's just not fair; Babe Ruth's father never
had to go through anything like this. "You want to try it a while
longer? Maybe you'll change your mind. You're really good at it."

"Nah. I want to play soccer instead."

Soccer? That is the unkindest cut of all. Can my only son be a
communist? *"Et tu,* Pelé?" I say, unfortunately out loud.

"Huh?"

"Nothing. Soccer could be fun, unless you like scoring, or
knowing how much time is left in the game, and if you don't
care about having to say words like 'nil.' Let's talk to Mom
about it."

"So you're not mad?" he asks.

"Of course not," I say, not mentioning that I'm pained, crushed,
and horrified.

When we get home, Laurie is watching the local news, which
has been heavily covering the Downey murder. The media apparently considers near beheadings sexy; if Downey had been
shot, it would have been a one-day story.

I don't talk to Laurie about Ricky's baseball-soccer decision,
because the coverage has given me an idea. And to make it
work, I need to go drink some beer.

Raymond Healy was feeling the pressure from his money people. They were technically his partners, but that's not how he thought of them. Theirs was a partnership of profit, or at least that was how it had been so far. If that profit ceased to exist, then so would the relationship.

Healy's other partner, Hendrik Cronje, had learned that lesson the hard way. The last time they had met, in Johannesburg, had been the last time they would ever meet.

Cronje had attempted to cheat Healy; in fact, he did more than make the attempt. He had absolutely cheated him, providing less merchandise than he was contracted and paid to provide. He either thought Healy would not notice, or would simply accept the situation as a cost of doing business.

Healy did neither. He handled Cronje the same way he had handled many enemies in his past, by shooting him in the head. And Cronje had reacted in the exact same way the other enemies had reacted, by dying.

Killing him was impulsive and counterproductive, but Healy had compounded the mistake by making an even bigger one. He had neglected to get rid of the body. It had been a thought-out decision; he reasoned that it would spread the word that

Healy was a very dangerous man, so that others would not mess with him in the future.

He had miscalculated. Those that would have replaced Cronje as a source worried that doing so could eventually mean sharing his fate. Cronje was no more unscrupulous than they were, in fact probably less so, which led them to the inescapable conclusion that doing business with Healy was not in their self-interest. And they were people who were one hundred percent motivated by self-interest.

They dealt in diamonds, as precious a commodity as existed, and there was no shortage of customers. Why deal with Healy when other, far less menacing people would fit the bill nicely?

So Healy was left in the very uncomfortable position of having to supply goods that he could not acquire, at a time when they were particularly needed. The people waiting for the goods were very dangerous, but that was not Healy's major concern. He was dangerous himself, as they would find out if they threatened him.

But this was a rare opportunity, a chance to make a score so big that it could easily be the final one. So what bothered Healy was that without the goods, without the diamonds, he would be deprived of a fortune.

Which was why he had to find Eric Brantley.

Well, look who's here. . . . Welcome to another episode of *Father Knows Best.*"
Vince Sanders, who doubles as my friend and the single most disagreeable person on the planet, is insulting me before I even get to the table. It's not a news event that he and Pete Stanton are at our regular table at Charlie's sports bar; it would take an act of Congress to keep them away.

What Vince is alluding to is the fact that I have not been here as regularly as usual, and that I often cite fatherly responsibilities as the reason. Vince understands the importance of family; he just ranks it somewhat below beer and sports.

For Pete nothing ranks above sports, and he has his eyes glued to one of the TVs showing the Mets game. He ignores my arrival, and I have to say I prefer that approach to Vince's.

"What a treat to see you guys," I say, while signaling to our waitress. I don't have to tell her what I want; she knows the drill. Light beer, hamburger, and French fries so burnt that it would take a forensics team from *CSI: Paris* to identify them.

"Mets stink," Pete says, ever the conversationalist.

"So Vince, I want to talk business with you." Vince is the managing editor of the *Record,* a local newspaper.

"Then make an appointment with my secretary. I think I have an opening a month from Wednesday."

"Good, that'll give you almost five weeks to read the story on the front page of the *Star Ledger.*"

Vince stares a dagger at me. "You threatening me?"

I nod. "Yup, and I'll go a step further. You listen to what I have to say, or I won't pick up the check."

He thinks for a moment, then looks at his watch and says, "I think a spot just opened up on my calendar . . . in four seconds. Talk to me."

"Gerry Downey stole one of our dogs an hour and a half before he died. The dog was sitting next to his body when we found him."

Pete frowns, and without taking his eyes off the television, says, "The dog thing again?"

I don't bother answering him, and Vince doesn't either. I've got his attention.

"Details," he says. "Give me details."

So I give him the details, at least as many as I have. I end my recounting of the events with, "And showing no concern for my own well-being, I rushed in to save the poor, innocent dog, even though I had every reason to believe I would have to deal with a vicious murderer."

Pete grunts his disgust, but my eyes are on Vince. As a good newspaperman, I know this will be irresistible to him. Downey's murder is a big local story, but it will lose steam, like all stories. This will present a fresh aspect of the case, and something that Vince's competitors won't have. It will give him a day or two advantage.

"And your interest in this is what exactly?" he asks.

"I want to find the dog's real owner."

Pete moves smoothly from a grunt to a moan, but he's having no impact on our conversation.

"Why?" Vince asks.

"Because I want to know if the theft of the dog is related to the murder."

"You representing the killer?" Vince asks.

"I'm representing the accused, at least through the arraignment."

Pete does a double take at this, and for the first time takes his eyes off the ball game. "You run out of ambulances to chase?"

"Actually, what I am doing is pursuing a line of inquiry that you seem to have missed. It's not the first time."

He shakes his head. "This isn't about dogs, it's about precious stones."

"What does that mean?"

"Downey had a pair of large uncut diamonds hidden in a drawer. Unless he was planning to get engaged to two women really soon, that's an unusual piece of information, don't you think?"

It's a very unusual piece of information, but I don't want to give him the satisfaction of my saying so, so instead I ignore him and turn to Vince. "What do you say, Vince?"

"You got pictures?"

"I've got a picture of the dog, Cheyenne. You printing it is how we're going to find the owner."

"And you'll give us an exclusive interview?"

"Of course I will. You're my favorite journalist."

He points to the food and drink on the table. "And you're picking up the check? Because I'm looking to have at least three more beers."

I nod. "Nothing would make me happier."

Vince smiles, something he only does when he knows he will not have to reach for his wallet. "I like your style."

W hat Eric Brantley felt was a combination of panic and despair. He was a smart guy, always had been. And not just smart as a chemist and scientist; that was something he was born with. He also considered himself smart when it came to common sense and living life. Yet it was that intelligence that had failed him.

And, he knew, one way or another, it would prove his undoing.

The murder of Gerry Downey had shaken him to his core, even more than the murder of Michael Caruso. Eric had known he was entering a world that could be dangerous, but the chance for astonishing wealth made it a risk that seemed worth taking. Because he was smart, and because he had the goods that he knew were so valuable, he thought he could handle it.

Caruso's murder, while horrifying, had somehow seemed within the realm of possibility. Of course it had stunned Eric, but not like the Downey killing. That had told him that his pursuers were relentless, and absolutely brutal. They would do anything to find him, and when they did, his life would be over.

Going to Downey in the first place was a major risk, and ultimately a major mistake. Nobody else could possibly understand, but with the loneliness and desolation he felt, he just wanted his dog with him. But he had misjudged the risk and that mistake had almost gotten him caught, and it had probably cost Downey his life.

But Eric believed that there was simply nothing he could now do. To go to the authorities would end his life in another way. He would go to prison on a number of charges, possibly including terrorism and murder. He might be killed in prison, but at the very least it was not a life that would be worth living.

So he had moved to this small town, to the state he had visited with his parents every summer. He had grown a beard, and was living a quiet, anonymous life, with no attachments. He knew that he was not far from where the incident was to take place; he had overheard them talking about it.

Logically, there was no way his pursuers could know where he was; this might have been the last place they'd look. Yet Eric knew in his gut that eventually they would find out. And then they would come for him.

They knew his secret, and worse yet, he knew theirs.

And he would take them both to his grave.

W hy don't one of you guys get the paper?"

I'm still in bed, speaking to Tara and Sebastian, who are lying on their dog beds across the room. Laurie is up already, probably hanging out with Ricky. The dogs and I are sleeping in, if that's how you can describe getting up at seven a.m.

Unfortunately, they are not finished with the sleeping part of their day. Sebastian ignores me entirely, while Tara briefly raises her eyes in a gesture of disdain. They would have no interest in trudging outside to get the paper under any circumstances, but at this hour of the morning they do not deem it worthy of serious consideration.

And then, as proof that dreams can come true, Laurie comes into the bedroom bearing a cup of coffee and the newspaper, both of which she hands to me. I accept both, and then say to Tara and Sebastian, "That is how I am supposed to be treated. You have much to learn from your human mother."

"I just thought you'd never get your ass out of bed," Laurie says. "Vince really came through."

I'm glad to hear that, and it is the reason I wanted to get the paper in the first place. "Great," I say, and I don't have to look hard to find out what she means. There, on page one, is the picture of Cheyenne that Willie had taken for the occasion.

The matching story has the headline, "Do you know this dog?" It then goes on to explain Cheyenne's connection to the Downey murder, and implies that the dog's identity might well be a key to solving the murder. The police, of course, consider the murder already solved, but Vince's reporter subtly implies that this new lead has the potential to prove them wrong.

"We hear from Sam yet?" I ask, and then realize that we couldn't have, because the phone would have woken me.

Before Laurie can respond, as if on cue, the phone starts ringing. She picks it up, looks at the caller ID, and hands it to me. "Speak of the computer devil," she says.

"What's up?" I ask when I answer it.

"Calls have started already," he says.

I had asked Vince to publish a phone number for people with information about Cheyenne to call, and he had done so. It's a number we got just for this purpose, and had installed in Sam's office. "The team in place?" I ask.

"All except for Morris. His great-grandkids are visiting; they go back to Pennsylvania tomorrow morning."

Sam teaches a computer class at the Wayne WMHA, and he has some prize students that he calls on occasionally to do some outside work. They include Hilda and Eli Mandlebaum, Leon Goldberg, and Morris Fishman. Hilda is the baby of the group, and Sam told me she's eighty-five. But they are smart, available, and they can outwork anyone. Plus, they get up at four-thirty in the morning, so by seven-thirty they are into the meat of the day.

"Anything promising so far?" I ask.

"I don't think so, but there have only been two calls. We're just taking down the information, and we'll analyze what we've got later. I'll be able to go over it with you tonight."

"Can we do that here? Laurie is teaching a class tonight, so I need to be here for Ricky."

"You angling for Father of the Year?" Sam asks.

"You think it's unusual that I would not want to leave an eight-year-old boy alone?"

"My parents left me alone all the time."

"Ahhh," I say. "Another piece of the puzzle slips neatly into place."

I reluctantly get out of bed, and take Tara and Sebastian on their morning walk, kissing Ricky and Laurie on the way out. My morning kissing output has doubled since Ricky entered our lives, but I'm okay with it.

We take a long walk through Eastside Park. Tara is very familiar with the route, and Sebastian is getting used to it, but both of them seem really into it. Tara sniffs something, and then Sebastian follows her lead, as if relying on Tara to point out the best stuff.

When we get home I call Billy "Bulldog" Cameron, the attorney who runs the public defender's office in Passaic County. He's not called Bulldog because he's a relentless defender of his clients, although he certainly is that. The nickname comes from the fact that he played football for Georgia, and famously caught a last-second pass to beat Auburn.

The other thing Billy is famous for is always complaining about how overworked and underpaid his meager office staff is. I let him do so for the first three minutes of the conversation, partially because his complaints are justified, and partially because I couldn't stop him if I tried.

He finally gets around to asking why I'm calling.

"I've got a client for you," I say. "A murder case."

"Just what I need. Why can't you represent him?"

"I am, but only through the arraignment, which is today. I'm doing it sort of as a favor."

"Well, how about doing me a favor?" he asks. "Extend your representation through the trial, conviction, sentencing, and execution."

"Sorry, I'm retiring. I'll invite you to the party; you can bring a gift. I'm registered at Tiffany's and Giants Stadium."

Billy agrees to have one of his attorneys, Deb Kohl, meet me at the arraignment, so I can introduce her to Tommy, and make the changeover.

I'm not even feeling guilty about it; I know Deb and she's talented and aggressive. She's in the public defender's office to help the most vulnerable in our society, which means she must have forgotten to take the Glory of Compensation in law school.

I've got a few hours before the arraignment, so I decide to browse through some of the discovery documents that the prosecutor's office on the Infante case has sent me. They are not aware that I am giving up the case after the arraignment, which means they clearly have me confused with someone with a work ethic.

It's only the very beginning of the case, but the prosecution already has some pretty strong evidence. They're aware of Tommy's admission that he helped Downey on the liquor store robbery, and also know of his threat to slit Downey's throat.

Maybe worse, the bloody knife that they believe killed Downey was found buried in Tommy's backyard. The tests have not come back yet to identify it as Downey's blood, but at this point it seems like a safe bet. There's also a whole bunch of fingerprint evidence.

All in all, it seems very much like a case I have no desire to try in front of a judge. Or a jury. Or a mirror.

I get to the courthouse a half hour early so I can meet with my soon-to-be ex-client. He's waiting for me in the anteroom when I get there, and the look on his face is familiar, one that I see in many clients when they make this first appearance in court. It's a combination of hope and fear.

He's been waiting for something, anything, to happen, and he's trying to believe that whatever is going to happen will be good. Someone is paying attention to him, and maybe that attention will somehow result in his going free.

Of course, the fear is very present as well. He's feeling intimidated by the process, and it is quite possible, even likely, that the full force of the government is about to commence squashing him.

What will soon become readily apparent to him is that arraignments are almost never of consequence. It's a way for the system to get its house in order as it relates to this particular case, just a setting of the judicial table.

I tell all this to Tommy, but I don't think it fully registers with him. He has no criminal record, which surprised me when I found out about it, but that means this is his first time going through this. Once the judge gets into the courtroom and starts droning on, he'll get the drift, but he's not ready for it yet.

"How do you want to plead?" I ask, and then explain the various options. The explanation doesn't take too long, since he's familiar with the concepts of "guilty" and "not guilty." I don't get into the plea bargaining possibilities, since I haven't discussed them with the prosecution. That will be for his next lawyer.

"Not guilty," he says.

"They found the probable murder weapon buried in the yard

behind your house." I'm not saying this to get him to change his plea; even if he is ultimately going to bargain, this is not the time to do anything but register a "not guilty" plea.

He does a double take in obvious surprise, or it could be a fake double take in fake surprise. "That can't be," he says. "They must have planted it. Damn . . . what can we do about it?"

"That will be for you to take up with your next lawyer. She'll be here and you'll meet her after the arraignment. Her name is Deb Kohl; I know her and she's good."

"I want you," he says, then more softly. "Please."

I start to answer, when the guard knocks on the door, and enters. "They're ready for you," he says.

We get up to head into the courtroom, and the guard walks ahead. "Do you have any idea why Downey would have two valuable diamonds in his apartment?" I ask.

Tommy looks puzzled. "Are you kidding? The son of a bitch told me he was broke."

Flying from the Republic of Georgia to New York is not an easy trip. The quickest way to do it is to fly out of Tbilisi Airport in Georgia, change planes in Moscow, and fly direct to JFK, but even that takes seventeen hours.

Alek didn't take the easiest way. One reason was that every member of the Russian military, as well as every law enforcement officer, would make their career by putting a bullet in his head. So Moscow was out.

But the other reason was that Alek needed deception and anonymity when he traveled; it was the only way he could get in and out of countries, especially the United States. Part of that process called for his flight into the United States to be from a friendly country, so in this case Alek's itinerary took him from Tbilisi, to Istanbul, to Frankfurt, to Madrid, and then to JFK.

For each leg of the trip, Alek traveled under a different name and nationality; his various identification documents had been expensive but perfectly prepared. At no time did he use his real name, although by this point in his thirty-four-year-old life he barely remembered what that real name was. His full first name was Aleksandre, but he was known by everyone simply as Alek.

No one had ever questioned him as to what his real full name was; Alek was not a person people questioned. He was a person people feared.

This particular trip to New York took forty-one hours, including a night in a hotel in Madrid. The final leg to New York was delayed two hours, so Alek arrived at three o'clock in the afternoon. He was not tired; being tired was not a luxury that he ever allowed himself.

The only way to describe his demeanor, the only way to ever describe it, was to say that he was alert. And very dangerous.

Alek took a cab into Manhattan, directing the driver to the Michelangelo Hotel, on Fifty-first Street between Sixth and Seventh Avenues. He had reserved a large suite; at this stage of his life, comfort was incongruously important to him. And compared to what he would earn for this operation, fourteen hundred dollars a night for the suite was a rounding error.

It was Alek's third time in New York, and if he had never come back, that would have been fine with him. He liked the energy, but not the people. He mocked the fact that New Yorkers considered themselves tough. Let them grow up where Alek grew up, and then they could talk about tough.

Once he checked into the hotel, Alek went outside to walk around, and to find some food to bring back to his room. He searched the faces of the people he saw, because that was what he was trained to do. But he saw no one that he recognized; nor did he expect to.

Alek would meet with his associate the next day, and it was then that he would fully assess the situation, and decide who he would have to kill. It would likely be a person who was himself dangerous; he would not die easily, but he would die. Perhaps he was going to have more than one target; that would be no problem either way.

He would have much preferred not to have to intervene like this, but time was of the essence, and the operation was far too unique and important to be compromised. Alek would see to it that it wasn't.

One thing was certain: if Alek wanted people dead, then those people would be dead. No matter what. No matter who.

Judge Lester Klingman will be presiding, and he is more than competent for the task at hand. Of course, Lance Ito could handle this proceeding without screwing it up. All he has to be able to do is ask a few questions, the same ones he's asked a thousand times before, and know how to read a calendar.

The fact that Judge Klingman is running the show today does not necessarily mean he will be the trial judge. It simply means he got stuck with the temporary short straw; he won't necessarily preside later on, although there is a definite chance that he will.

It is a sign of how little attention I've been paying to this case that I haven't even bothered to discover who is handling matters on the prosecution side. Once in the courtroom I see that it is Dylan Campbell, a smart, tough, arrogant, obnoxious attorney who I have beaten twice in major cases, and who therefore hates everything about me.

There is no doubt in my mind that Dylan is using his position as a jumping-off point to a hoped-for political career, and it is possible that his two very public losses to me could have slowed that train down somewhat. If so, I'm fine with that.

Dylan comes over and insincerely shakes my hand and welcomes me to the case. "You might want to plead this one out," he says. "If I let you."

I smile. "My recollection is that you said the same thing last time. And the time before that. Lucky for my clients they went to trial, huh?"

His smile is fake. "Yesterday's news. And the word is you're turning it over to Bulldog's people. Which may be why Kohl is here?"

He points toward Deb Kohl sitting two rows behind the defense table. "She'll kick your ass," I say, and then head back to my spot at the defense table.

I sit next to Tommy, and Judge Klingman enters the courtroom. We listen to him describe the situation as it stands and ask Dylan if he has any motions to present that are not in the record. He does not.

Then the judge asks me if we are ready to enter a plea, and I say that we are. I'm going to leave my withdrawal from the case until the end of the proceeding. I expect a little pushback from Judge Klingman, but not much. A murder case is a daunting undertaking, and if I don't want to do it, he won't try to coerce me. Especially since I have a competent replacement waiting in the judicial wings.

There is a decent crowd in the gallery, and quite a few media people. It was a particularly brutal murder, and throat slicing sells. Since I'm going to be slinking off, I'm not pleased that the press will cover it, but it is what it is. I'm a big boy and I can handle it, and if any reporters are particularly mean, I'll ask Laurie to beat them up.

Tommy and I stand, and the judge asks him how he pleads. He says not guilty, with a touch of shakiness in his voice. His nervousness is very understandable.

The judge takes a few moments to examine the court calendar, so as to set a date for trial. He comes up with one, and the prosecution and I both tentatively agree to it. If I were handling the case I would think it is too soon, but Deb and her client may feel differently. In any event, when she comes on board she will be able to push it back, if that is what she decides.

This thing is wrapping up, and I say, "Your Honor, there is one more item we would like to bring up for the court's consideration." I'm about to utter my exit line, when I notice that Sam has entered the courtroom.

He is signaling to me, trying to get my attention, and it seems urgent enough that I ask the judge for a moment so that I can consult with my "assistant." Things have moved smoothly enough that Klingman obligingly grants my request, though he could have given me a hard time about it.

Sam comes to the defense table, and we talk softly so that no one can hear. "Sam, what is it?"

He seems excited about something. "We found out whose dog it is."

"Good. Can we talk about it later?"

"I thought you'd want to know, and Laurie said I should get down here and tell you right away."

Laurie's involvement in this is surprising: she of all people knows that courtroom proceedings are not to be interrupted. "Okay, so tell me. Whose dog is it?"

"Eric Brantley."

"*The* Eric Brantley?"

He nods. "Yup. I'm positive."

I'm about to question him on how he can be so sure, when I hear the judge speaking to me from the bench. "Mr. Carpenter, we're all waiting."

I turn back toward him, making a decision while I do so.

Unfortunately, based on what comes out of my mouth, I'm obviously not a good decision maker while turning. "We don't have anything to bring up after all, Judge. Sorry to delay things."

The judge frowns slightly and adjourns the proceedings. I can see that Tommy is surprised I didn't withdraw as his lawyer, and I have no doubt that Deb Kohl shares his confusion. Dylan's face is impassive, but he must be unsure what the hell is going on.

But none of them know what I know.

That this case just got a hell of a lot more interesting.

Gerald Downey's murder knocked Eric Brantley out of the headlines. Ten days ago, Brantley's business partner, Michael Caruso, was found murdered in Brantley's house, the victim of a bullet in the back of the head. The two men, both research chemists, had left their place of employment at Markham College just weeks before, ostensibly to start their own company.

Brantley has not been found, and has been identified by police as the suspect in the killing. Information, at least the information available to the public, has been limited, but that has not deterred, and has in fact increased, speculation.

Rumors abound, and the motive has been called anything from a business dispute to an angry breakup between gay lovers. The fact that there is no evidence that either man was gay doesn't seem to have stopped the media from raising this possibility.

Of course, a good throat slicing will push a three-week-old shooting off the front page every day of the week, and Downey's murder proved to be no exception to that media rule. But what Sam has just told me indicates that the two killings might well be related.

As soon as Judge Klingman bangs his gavel Tommy turns to me and says, "What the hell is going on? What did he tell you?"

"We have information that the dog Downey stole was owned by Eric Brantley."

"The guy who murdered his partner?"

"I don't think a jury has decided on that yet. You might be familiar with the distinction." It's a pet peeve of mine that the public assumes the accused are guilty before trial. Even Tommy, who himself claims to be wrongly accused, has fallen into that trap.

He nods, understanding my not-very-subtle point. "Got it. But what does it mean for me?"

"I don't know; maybe nothing. But it's interesting enough to make me want to find out. Unless you want to bring Deb on board now; that's your absolute right."

He doesn't hesitate. "I'll stick with you, as long as you're in for good."

Sam is waiting for me, but first I stop and talk to Deb. I tell her what's happening without getting into specifics. Then I apologize for wasting her time, but she's fine with it. She probably has twenty other cases to handle, so missing out on this one is her preferred outcome.

When I finally get to Sam, I ask, "Where are we going?"

"The foundation."

"Drive with me," I say. "We can pick up your car later."

On the way I ask Sam to tell me how he can be so sure that Cheyenne is Eric Brantley's dog.

"Brantley's girlfriend sent me two pictures of Brantley with the dog."

"Pictures? That's it? It's a shepherd mix. Do you have any idea how many dogs look just like that?"

He's adamant. "This is the same dog. The pictures are identical, and if you heard her talking about it, you'd believe her also."

This is a potential nightmare; did I just take on a murder case based on this? Am I that stupid? "Sam," I say, "the issue is not whether she believes it's the same dog. I'm sure she does. The issue is whether she is right, simply by looking at a newspaper photograph."

"Trust me on this, Andy."

"And Laurie told you to interrupt the hearing to tell me this information?"

"Well, she didn't say interrupt the hearing. She just said to tell you about it right away."

I have nothing else to say, so I just moan.

"We'll find out soon enough," Sam says. "She's meeting us at the foundation. By the way, the dog's name is Zoe."

Zoe?

As we arrive at the foundation, which is on Route 20, another car pulls up, and a woman gets out. She is in sweatshirt and sweatpants, wearing a baseball cap with her hair pulled through it in the back. She looks like she just came from working out, but she doesn't look tired. She looks excited.

"Sam?"

"That's me," Sam says. "This is Andy. Andy, this is Stephanie Manning."

We exchange hellos, and then she asks, "Is Zoe inside?"

Before either of us can answer, she's heading for the door. She opens it and walks in, and we follow her. We have a large play area in the center of the building, where potential adopters can hang out and play with the dogs they are interested in. Willie often brings five or six dogs out there at a time, and he throws a ball with them.

That's what he's doing now, and one of the dogs he's playing with is the dog we named Cheyenne. Willie is facing us, and the dogs are facing him, which means they are not looking at us.

Stephanie yells out, "ZOE!"

All of the dogs turn around, just from the surprise of hearing the sound behind them. But Cheyenne does something the others do not do: she takes one look at Stephanie and races toward her, tail wagging as fast as she can wag it. When she reaches her, she jumps on her, and human and dog start rolling around on the floor.

"I told you," Sam says. "It's Eric Brantley's dog."

I nod. "Yes, you did, and yes, it is."

Stephanie plays with her for another five minutes or so, and then we go into the office. Zoe comes with us, because none of us would have the courage or ability to separate her from Stephanie.

I have a lot of questions for her, but she asks the first one. "How did you get her?"

"Animal control found her running stray. They took her to the shelter, and when no one showed up to claim her, we took her."

"Why?"

"Because she was in danger." What I don't say is that she was likely to be euthanized.

Now it's my turn. "Do you know how she came to be lost?"

Stephanie shakes her head. "No, I assumed that she was with Eric, wherever he is."

"Why?"

"Because he loves her as much as anyone could love anything. It's not possible that he went somewhere willingly without her."

She knows all about Gerry Downey's stealing Zoe, and his subsequent murder, from the article in the paper. I ask her if she has any idea at all why Downey would have taken her, but she claims she doesn't, and I believe her.

"Zoe had no tag and no collar. Does that surprise you?"

She shakes her head. "No, I always talked to Eric about that, but he never put one on her. I know it's stupid, but I think he considered it demeaning to her, like it made it seem she was a possession or something."

"Can I ask what your relationship with Eric is?"

She hesitates. "We've been dating for almost two years." Then she smiles, as if embarrassed, and says, "We joke that we're engaged to be engaged."

I don't ask Stephanie if she knows where Brantley is, because she no doubt wouldn't tell me if she did. And I don't ask her if she thinks he killed his partner, but she volunteers her opinion anyway.

"They couldn't be more wrong about Eric," she says. "He could never kill anyone. He could never even hurt anyone, especially Michael. They were best friends as well as partners."

"What kind of business were they in?"

"They were incredibly smart," she says, which doesn't really answer the question. Then she corrects herself, not wanting to talk about Brantley in the past tense. "Eric *is* incredibly smart. Whatever they were doing, it would have been successful."

"You don't know what they were doing?"

"I don't, no. It was a secret, even from me."

We talk some more, but she seems to have nothing to add. "I'd like to take Zoe home to my house," she says.

I knew that might come up, and had thought about it. "No, that wouldn't be a good idea. If Downey stole her, then someone else might try to do the same. It could be dangerous for you."

Legally I have every right to keep Zoe; we got her from the shelter by paying a fee. The only person we have any obligation to would be the actual owner, and that obligation would be more moral than legal. But it doesn't matter, because Stephanie is not the owner.

I expect her to push back, but she nods her understanding. "Can I come visit her?"

"Sure," I say. "We'll make arrangements with Willie."

Willie seems unconcerned about the possibility that another attempt might be made to steal Zoe. I know this because when I raise the possibility, he says, "I hope they do." Willie is not really the fearful type, and this is an example of the difference between him and me, because I definitely hope they don't.

But he is the protective type, and he understands the potential danger to Sondra. For that reason he says that Zoe will be with him 24-7; wherever he goes, she will go.

I'm trying to make sense out of the whole situation, and figure out how to use it to my client's advantage. The most logical explanation would be that Brantley murdered his partner, Michael Caruso, and then went on the run.

For whatever reason, probably because he panicked, or feared imminent capture, he left quickly and wasn't able to take his dog. But he loved Zoe, and wanted to reunite with her. Somehow she had gotten lost in the process, and gone to the shelter, and then to us.

But he didn't want to reveal himself to us, perhaps even realizing who I was, and that I might be tied in enough to law enforcement community happenings to recognize him. Of course, anyone had the obvious potential to do so, since his photo was frequently broadcast on the local news. So he contracted with Downey to steal Zoe and bring her to him.

But this is where the logical explanation turns illogical. Once Downey got the dog, then Brantley would either have come to get her, or sent someone to do so. But why would Brantley or the other person have killed Downey? Maybe an argument over money? Maybe Downey was holding the dog for a sort of ransom, not wanting to turn her over unless Brantley upped the ante?

But why would Brantley, or his emissary, possibly have left Zoe behind? If my theory was correct, then Zoe was the sole reason Downey was involved in this in the first place. Could it be that the killer panicked when Pete, Willie, and I arrived on the scene? Might Brantley have escaped without his dog for a second time?

One thing I am simply not about to consider is the possibility of coincidence, that maybe Downey stole Zoe and was then murdered by someone for reasons that had nothing to do with her. The idea that one dog could be involved in two unrelated murders within two weeks is simply not remotely possible, at least in my eyes.

Perhaps even more important than the question of what the hell is going on is what the hell I'm going to do with it. Because it currently makes no sense, I don't really know which way it cuts. Is it in my client's interest to be even peripherally connected to Brantley, whom the cops consider a murderer?

I've also noticed, to my distress, that I have started thinking of Tommy as my client. I want a client as much as I want a four-hour enema, but it is neither professional nor fair to bounce Tommy around like a legal rubber ball. If I was going to bail out on him, and I was, it should have been at the arraignment.

Sam's information made me blink and shy away from backing out of the case. That was not Tommy's fault, and he shouldn't suffer for it.

As Michael Corleone said in *The Godfather, Part III,* "Just when I thought I was out, they pull me back in." The fact that it was the worst movie in the history of movies does not take away from the truth of that statement, as it relates to my legal career.

I'm starting to think it's in my client's best interest for law enforcement to know what I know about the Brantley connection. In a perfect world, I would go to the prosecutor, since the police involvement in our case mostly ended with the arrest.

But with Dylan as the prosecutor, the world is far from perfect. I don't trust him to be interested in looking for exculpatory evidence, and I think he would try to either ignore or minimize the significance of what I'd be telling him. He is not a viable option.

Which leaves Pete. "I need to see you," I say, when I get him on the phone.

"Are we dating?" he asks.

"That is a truly chilling thought. But I do need to see you."

"When?"

"Tonight," I say. "It's important." It doesn't really have to be tonight, but I feel guilty that I haven't been aggressive on Tommy's behalf until now, and I want to rectify that. I also want Pete to understand that I consider this very significant information.

"Okay. I'll see you at Charlie's."

"I can't. Laurie is teaching a class tonight, so I have to take care of Ricky."

"Bring him to Charlie's."

"It's a school night," I say.

"Not for me."

"Come on, I'll bring in a pizza."

"Who the hell are you?" he asks. "Mr. Mom? What's next? You going to move to the suburbs and do ironing and shit?"

"Just come over."

"What's it about this time? A missing pussycat?"

I put up with a few more insults, and he agrees to come by the house. I head home, and when I arrive I have to fight off the urge I've been having lately to yell, "Honey! Ricky! I'm home!"

Coming home to a family is different from coming home to just Laurie used to be. I think I like this new situation better, but it sort of makes me feel more mature than I want to be. It's like I should light up a pipe and head to the den to read the evening paper.

We all sit down to dinner, but I don't mention the pizza that will soon be making an appearance in this very kitchen. When we're done, I quickly explain to Laurie what is going on.

"So you are taking Infante on as a client?" she asks.

"I think I should."

"Of course you should. But you're actually going to?"

"Yes; it's the right thing to do."

She smiles a great smile, and turns to Ricky. "Our little Andy is growing up."

When Pete arrives, I have him watch Ricky while I pick up the pizza. He seems a little uncomfortable with the idea; Pete probably hasn't been alone in a room with a nine-year-old since he was that age himself. But Pete and Ricky know each other very well; Pete was close with Ricky's real father.

"What should I do?" he asks.

"Maybe he'll be doing some homework, so you can learn something. And you can call in backup in case he starts to beat you up, right?"

I go out to get the pizza, just cheese, no toppings, the way the Pizza God intended. The number of toppings that they put on pizza these days is getting out of hand; Laurie turns it into a goddamn salad. Somebody has to step up and say enough is enough, and I'm the man for the job.

When I get back home, I see that Pete is in the den with Ricky, playing Madden football on the large-screen TV. Homework seems not to be happening. "What's the score?" I ask.

"He's up two touchdowns and is on my four-yard line," Pete says.

"He's terrible," Ricky chimes in.

"Maybe we can talk at halftime in the locker room," I say.

Pete extricates himself from the game, though it's not due to my sarcasm. It's more the smell of the pizza. While he's chomping down his fourth slice, he asks, "What have you got?"

"You know that dog Cheyenne that was stolen and was with Downey when he got killed?"

"Of course I know about her; that's all you ever talk about. Where did she turn up this time? The White House?"

"Her real name is Zoe—"

He interrupts. "Wow. That changes everything."

"And she was owned by Eric Brantley."

He does a startled double take so sudden that for a second I'm afraid he might choke on the crust. "How do you know that?"

"Not important, but it's one hundred percent."

He seems to eye me warily. "You know where Brantley is?"

I shake my head. "No." Then, "What do you think this means?"

He thinks for a moment. "It's interesting."

"Say hallelujah," I say. "Sherlock Holmes lives."

We talk some more about it, but Pete has no more insight into it than I do, which is not a hell of a lot of insight. "I'm not running the Brantley case," he says. "You want me to share it with the detectives that are on it?"

"No harm in it," I say.

"Probably no help either. They're pretty sure the bad guy is Brantley, and I'm sure that Infante killed Downey. I don't see how the dog changes things."

"The dog changes everything," I say. "We just don't know how yet." Then, "Did you find out where Downey got those diamonds?"

He shakes his head. "Not yet. Best guess is he stole them . . . they're big stones."

"How much are they worth?"

"I have no idea, but they look sparkly to me. Downey must have had good taste. He had a good head off his shoulders."

"Now you're doing decapitation jokes?" I ask.

He shrugs. "How often do I get the chance?"

'm afraid I've got very little for you," Sam says. He's come over to give his report on his investigation into Downey's phone activity.

"I've got to tell you, Sam. That is not an upbeat way to open a conversation. For future reference, I prefer things like, 'Wait 'til you hear this, Andy,' or, 'Andy, you're gonna love what I found out.' "

"Sorry," Sam says, and I can tell he feels badly, so I back off.

"That's okay, just tell me what you learned."

"There was very little banking activity; if he received or sent any large amounts of money, it wasn't through normal channels."

This is interesting in and of itself, since Downey had those diamonds in his possession. He either paid in cash, or stole them, or maybe received them for services rendered. Of course, there's always the possibility they have been passed down through the Downey family since Nehemiah Downey mined them hundreds of years ago, but it doesn't help to consider that.

"Did he have the kind of money that would indicate he could have bought two large diamonds?" I ask.

"No way; he had twelve hundred dollars in the bank, and no

investments that I could find. He didn't own the house he lived in, and his car is six years old. Maybe the stones are fakes."

"What else?"

"I've got the phone numbers of the people he called, and those who called him. I've attached names to most of them, although he received some calls from a few of those noncontract phones, so there's no way to know who owned them."

"Anybody interesting on the list?"

He shrugs. "Hard to know, but it didn't seem like it. I've got the team on it, but they're just names, you know? Difficult to tell if they mean anything. We're going to start digging into each person to see what more we can find out."

"What about the GPS? Where was he?" I ask, knowing that Sam checked the GPS records on Downey's phone. He can technically only tell me where the phone was, not where Downey was, but the two are generally the same.

"No place special that I can see," Sam said. "He didn't attend a criminals' convention or anything. Hung out a lot in a bar on Market Street. He also spent a hell of a lot of time across the road from the foundation building, and he was definitely in there the evening he died."

What Sam is saying doesn't surprise me, but the fact that Downey so carefully staked out the building confirms the importance of his taking Zoe. It wasn't any kind of impulse; it was a carefully planned and executed robbery.

Sam leaves to go down to the office; we're going to have a meeting down there to officially get the team working on the case. I wait for Laurie to get home, and drive there with her, updating her on the way with what I know. It is a longer trip than necessary for that; I could tell her what I know in the time it takes to drive one block.

The group has already assembled when we arrive. In addition

to Sam and Willie, there is Edna, my secretary turned administrative assistant. She made the title change herself, and if either of the titles implies that she does any actual work, they are as inaccurate as if she called herself Governor Edna, or Astronaut Edna.

Also here for the meeting is Hike Lynch, my associate, a brilliant lawyer with the uncanny ability to see the negative in everything. Next to him is Marcus, which means that Hike was the last to arrive. No one would willingly take a seat next to Marcus; except for Laurie, they would all be too afraid.

Laurie seems somehow exempt from the "fear of Marcus" syndrome, and she takes the chair on his other side. As always, he greets her, and only her, with a small smile.

Marcus is an outstanding investigator, which fortunately puts him on Laurie's team. The only dealings I have with him are when he is called on to perform the vital task of preventing me from getting killed. He is extraordinarily good at that, since when it comes to toughness, he makes Luca Brasi look like Fredo.

I outline the parameters of the case to the team, telling them what we know so far. "We have one client, but we're investigating two murders," I say. "And I don't believe that the answers will be found in the Downey murder. Even though that's the one our client is charged with, I think the key is the murder of Michael Caruso, in which Eric Brantley is the suspect.

"The two killings are tied together by a dog. She was owned by a murder suspect, and stolen by someone else, a few minutes before the thief became a murder victim himself. That is not a coincidence; there is a definite connection, and we have to find the link."

"How strong a case do they have against Brantley?" Hike asks.

"I don't know," I say. "They think it's strong, but they've been wrong before. Just like they're going to be wrong about Tommy Infante."

"So you think Brantley is innocent?"

"Could be."

Hike laughs. "Because of the dog, right? You think anyone who loves a dog that much must be a good guy."

I think about it for a minute and realize that Hike is not far off in his assessment. "Let's put it this way: someone will have to prove otherwise."

We kick things around a bit more, focusing on how we might find Brantley before the police do. Laurie says, "I think we should be watching Stephanie Manning. You said Zoe went crazy when she saw her, and a dog wouldn't act that way unless she spent a lot of time with her. Which leads to the obvious conclusion that she and Eric Brantley are very close."

"So you think she could lead us to him," I say, once again showing a mastery of the obvious.

"I do."

Since we have no one for Marcus to pound into a pulp at the moment, Laurie assigns him to watch Stephanie. It'll be a piece of cake for him. Even though Marcus is the scariest person in the western hemisphere, he has an amazing ability to go invisible when trailing someone.

"You okay with this, Marcus?" Laurie asks.

"Yuh," says Marcus, understating the case.

know very little about Markham College. That isn't typical of me; I actually know a great deal about many of our nation's finest academic institutions. For example, even though it's only April, I can tell you which school Notre Dame is playing in their opening game. And I can probably predict three of the Heisman finalists right now, though not a pass has yet been thrown.

The thing about Markham that keeps it off my radar is that it pretty much doesn't have a single team that I can bet on, or against. I'm not saying that reflects negatively on Markham as an institution; it is known for turning out leaders in fields as diverse as the sciences, math, engineering, and the arts.

That's all well and good, but it doesn't get you into a bowl game.

Of course, these days Markham is known for more than academic achievement and mediocre athletics. It has been plunged into the news in a way that this small northern New Jersey college has never been before. Markham may have turned out some very accomplished scholars, but right now none are as famous as Eric Brantley and the late Michael Caruso.

I'm here to see Professor Charles Horowitz, who runs the

chemistry department at Markham. He was the person that both Brantley and Caruso reported to, which means he has been besieged with interview requests from the media. I read somewhere that he has been turning them all down, so rather than call him direct and get shot down, I called Robby Divine.

I originally met Robby while sitting next to him at a charity dinner. I have almost thirty million dollars, much of it inherited, but if that much money slipped through a hole in Robby's pocket, he probably wouldn't notice it.

He's a multibillionaire and a graduate of Markham, but wealthy alums don't necessarily impress the Markham administrators. Wealthy alums who donate twenty million dollars to the school do make an impression, however, and that is the category that Robby falls into.

It's fair to say that they have an interest in keeping Robby happy, so when he called and said he would like Professor Horowitz to meet with me, the word made its way down to the good professor that he should do just that.

So he is. Today. But that doesn't mean he has to like it, and I'm expecting quite a bit of resistance. I'll probably be called on to use a significant amount of the Andy Carpenter charm. Fortunately I have it in ample supply.

If I called central casting and asked them to send down a chemistry professor, he would look nothing like Charles Horowitz. Horowitz is at least six foot six, maybe 190 pounds, and he can't be more than forty years old. He looks like he'd be more at home on a basketball court getting a rebound than hunched over a Bunsen burner or microscope or whatever the hell chemists hunch over.

"I hope this isn't about Eric Brantley," he says.

"Your hope is about to be dashed," I say.

"I've told the police everything I know, which isn't much."

"Then let's start not with what you know, but what you think. Do you think Brantley killed his partner?"

"No."

"Why not?"

"Just a feeling I have. I simply don't see him capable of that kind of violence. He and Michael were best friends, which makes it even harder to believe, but that's not what I base it on. It's just not Eric."

"Why did they leave their jobs? Were they fired?"

He thinks for a moment, though that shouldn't be that tough a question to answer. "Not really, though by the time Eric left, I would describe it as a mutual parting."

"What caused it?"

"I'm not really sure. Eric just seemed to lose interest in what he was supposed to be doing. His research work slacked off, as did his teaching. It was uncharacteristic, to say the least."

"Do you have any suspicions about what was going on?"

He nods. "I think both Eric and Michael were doing work not sanctioned by the university, which they chose to keep from me. They were here long hours, but the output that we were shown never corresponded to those hours."

"What kind of work did they specialize in?"

"Eric is both an organic and physical chemist, absolutely out-standing. We were lucky to have him as long as we did; he would have been welcomed at any institution, and certainly could have called his shot in private industry."

"And Caruso?"

"Talented, probably on my level, but not in Eric's league. Very few are in Eric's league."

I ask Horowitz the obligatory questions about whether he

has knowledge of Brantley's whereabouts, and he says that he doesn't. I believe him, though I'm certain he would not tell me if he did know.

As I'm about to leave, I ask, "Did you ever meet Eric's dog?"

Horowitz smiles. "Zoe? I certainly did; Eric made bringing the dog to work a condition of his employment. He loves that dog . . . she is very sweet. What happened to her?"

"Well, I would say she's been leading an interesting life."

For Stephanie Manning, things had gone from horrifying to surreal. First came the news that Michael Caruso was murdered. She had met Michael a bunch of times, of course through Eric, but really didn't know him that well. Eric didn't talk about his work much, and Stephanie always assumed that was because he correctly gauged that she wouldn't understand any of it.

But Stephanie had never been connected to any kind of violence like that. A distant cousin of hers had once been raped, but Stephanie was just ten at the time, and she hadn't really fully understood the implications. She also had never met the cousin, so she wasn't emotionally impacted by it.

Then, right on the heels of the news about Michael was the revelation that Eric was a suspect. She just assumed that it was a terrible mistake, and that he would explain things to the authorities in a way that would clear him.

Following that, the third of a three-punch devastating combination was learning that Eric was missing. That's not how the police characterized it; "missing" implied that he might somehow also be a victim. It was clear they thought he had fled out of fear of prosecution.

But Stephanie didn't believe it, not for a second. Eric was innocent; Michael was his closest friend in the world, her excluded. In fact, they were two of the only friends that Eric, a true loner, had. That, coupled with the fact that Eric was as gentle a soul as she had ever met, precluded his guilt. It made no sense that he would run, rather than stay and prove his innocence.

So the truth, she feared, had to be worse. Whoever had killed Michael must have been after Eric as well, and either captured him, killed him, or caused him to go into hiding.

Stephanie was a logical person, and could not hide from the fact that Eric's being in hiding made little sense. He shouldn't be so afraid of the people that killed Michael that he'd need to run; if he turned himself in to the police, and told what he knew, he would be protected.

So every day the situation grew more frightening, and more surreal. Just seeing Eric's picture on every newscast, with the announcers talking about him like he was a murderer, was hard for her to process as reality.

But if Eric was okay, then he was watching those newscasts as well, and he was not reaching out to anyone. Not the authorities. Not Stephanie.

Stephanie stayed home as much as she could; as a freelance features writer, her time was pretty much her own. She did not want to leave the phone, in case Eric called her. He had her cell number if she went out, but service in her area was occasionally spotty, and she didn't want to take a chance on missing his call.

So she was home when the UPS truck pulled up and the driver walked to her porch, carrying a small package. She signed for it and saw that the sender's name was Robert Boyle. It was a name that was vaguely familiar to her, but she couldn't place it.

She opened the package, and inside was another, smaller

package. She opened that as well, and took out a cell phone, the kind that you can buy at a store without signing a contract.

Stephanie's hand started to shake at the realization of what this meant, so much so that she had to steady herself to turn the phone on. She knew without a doubt that it was from Eric, and that meant that he was alive.

She also knew that he was going to contact her, but probably feared that her phones might be bugged. So he would call her on this phone, and he would explain everything.

All she had to do was wait.

Hike had filed the motion, and it should have been just a formality. But Dylan challenged it, for no other reason than that Dylan challenges everything.

That's why we're having this hearing in open court before Judge Klingman to decide the issue. Each side has explained their position in writing, and oral arguments should be brief.

"As we stated, Your Honor, we want a defense expert to examine the diamonds that were found in the victim's possession. The police confiscated them, which by definition means that they consider them possible evidence, and the defense is entitled to its own examination of all the evidence. As the court is no doubt aware, we are not exactly creating new law with this request; it is standard procedure."

The judge turns to Dylan. "Mr. Campbell?"

Dylan stands. "No one is questioning the defense's right to examine evidence, Your Honor. We are simply objecting to the timing; we have not even had time to examine it ourselves."

"Your Honor," I say, "the examination should not take more than a couple of hours. They've had three weeks."

"Three weeks is not a lot of time to examine all of the evidence in this case," Dylan says.

I nod and speak to the judge. "That's reasonable. So if the prosecution was planning to examine the diamonds today, we'll wait until tomorrow. If they were not going to do it today, then we'll take them and have them back tomorrow. That won't set them back at all."

Judge Klingman turns to Dylan. "Were you planning to have your experts examine the diamonds today?"

"No, Your Honor."

"Tomorrow?"

"Possibly," Dylan lies. The truth is he has no idea when they would do so; it may not even have been on their list of things to do.

"Perfect," I say, even though no one asked for my opinion. "We can go get them now, and we'll have them back tomorrow. Mr. Campbell can have one of his associates present for the examination if he likes. But we'll be quick, because the last thing we want to do is obstruct Mr. Campbell's schedule." I smile at Dylan, but he doesn't smile back.

"I'll sign the order," the judge says, and then continues, staring admonishingly at Dylan. "I think we're done here; we never should have had to be here in the first place."

I send Hike down to get the diamonds, and call Willie to have him meet Hike there. Hike is even less physical than I am, and if he's going to be carrying around two valuable stones, I want Willie nearby as protection. I had alerted Willie to this possibility, and he's going to bring Zoe with him. He doesn't want to leave her out of his sight, or leave Sondra alone with her.

I head back to the office to do some paperwork, and am surprised to see Laurie and Sam there. "What's up?" I ask, because I am the curious type.

"Marcus called in," Laurie says. "Stephanie Manning got a FedEx package."

"Do we know what was in it?"

She shakes her head. "We don't. But we know who and where it was from. Sam got it out of the FedEx computer."

"I suppose it's too much to hope it came from Eric Brantley?"

"That remains to be seen," she says, and Sam chimes in, "It was sent by Robert Boyle, from a UPS office in Brunswick, Maine. It was paid for in cash."

"Anything significant about that?" I ask.

"Robert Boyle is considered to be the first modern chemist," Laurie says.

"And he lives in Maine?"

"No, he died in the seventeenth century."

"And he's still sending packages?"

Laurie frowns at my attempts at humor. "Eric Brantley was a chemist. Stephanie Manning gets a FedEx from someone with a famous chemist's name, who paid in cash. It's certainly possible the sender was Brantley."

"I can put my team on it," Sam says. "We can check out all the Robert Boyles in the Brunswick area, and try to connect one of them to Stephanie Manning."

I nod. "Worth a try." It's a long shot, but at this point we have very few shots, and as long as the Mandlebaums and the gang don't mind doing the work, we've got nothing to lose.

But probably little to gain.

Harry Goldman mans one of what seems like three million jewelry counters on Forty-seventh Street in Manhattan. Actually, trying to navigate through it all, three million seems like something of an understatement. Because the setting is so modest, it's hard to believe that each of the cases under the counters is packed with valuable jewelry. It also seems hard to believe that there could be enough customers spending enough dollars to keep all these counter people in profit, but I'm sure there are, because they wouldn't be packed in here for their health.

I have to admit I don't understand the appeal of jewelry. I guess some of it is nice to look at, but it has a value only because we say it does. It's useless; you can't live in it, drive it, listen to it, eat it, drink it, or swim in it. But people pay out huge sums of money for these little rocks, and as they get more successful, they trade them in for bigger little rocks.

I doubt that I would have ever found Harry's counter if not for the fact that Hike, Willie, and Zoe are standing in front of it. I also doubt that dogs are allowed in here, but I'm positive that no one would have the nerve to tell that to Willie. Willie's not Marcus, but he projects a toughness that can be intimidating.

Dylan has not sent someone to be present at this examination; it confirms my feeling that he doesn't consider it important. He could easily be right about that.

Harry and I went to high school together, and we meet for lunch once every few months. He sold me the engagement ring I gave Laurie. He told me he gave me a deal on it, but a good guess is that he tells that to everyone. For what I paid, I could have gotten something with bucket seats and satellite radio.

I don't see too many people from the old days, since pretty much all of them have moved out of Paterson. So has Harry, but he lives nearby in Teaneck.

I've spent my adult years exaggerating my athletic and romantic exploits in high school, so with Harry I have to consciously remember that he knows the truth. Of course, he was no more successful than I was in those areas, so we basically avoid talking about them. Instead we talk about sports and *Seinfeld,* his two passions in life.

But there's no chitchatting today; I get right to the point. "What do you think about the stones?"

"I haven't looked at them yet. Your friends didn't want to give them to me until you showed up."

I nod to Hike, and he takes the stones out of his pocket and hands them to Harry, who lays a felt cloth on the counter and puts the stones on it. He stares at them for at least a minute, then nods slightly, though it's impossible to tell what that means.

"What is it you want to know?" he asks.

"Two things. How valuable they are, and if it's possible to trace where they came from."

Harry picks up the stones and brings them back to a small desk he has beyond the counter. He has some equipment that he uses to look at the stones, and strange little lights that he shines on them. The process takes about ten minutes, during which time he does not say a single word.

When he's finished, he carries the diamonds carefully back to the counter, still resting on the cloth, and puts them down in front of us. "Where did you get these?" he asks.

"From a murder victim."

"He's got good taste in stones. They're real, and they're spectacular."

It's a *Seinfeld*-ism, but I assume he means it seriously. "So they're valuable?"

"Probably a hundred and fifty grand each. Very unusual."

"Unusual how?" I ask.

"Outstanding grade and quality, but they're uncut and unregistered."

"So?"

"So you don't usually see uncut stones this small. Which means they're probably not blood diamonds. But they're unregistered, which means they might be."

"Blood diamonds" is a term I've heard; I even think there was a movie about them. But I don't know what it means, so I ask Harry to explain.

"They're diamonds usually mined in West Africa, in war zones. They're stolen and sent to other countries to finance war efforts, arms purchases, things like that. But they would generally be larger stones."

"Any way to trace these?" I ask.

He shakes his head. "Not really. There's no laser identification on them. That would come when they are cut. I know people that could probably tell you what country they were mined in, but that's as specific as they could get."

"How do I learn more about all of this?" I ask.

He thinks for a moment, and then says, "You know Alan Divac?"

"No."

"See if you can get to him. He is the go-to guy when it comes to bringing diamonds into the country. That diamond I sold you was one of his."

"So you know him?"

He shakes his head. "No, there are about twelve rungs between us on the ladder."

"But the diamonds he brings in are legal?"

He shrugs. "Depends on who you talk to."

I thank him, and as we're ready to leave, he points to the evidence diamonds and asks, "Are these yours to sell?"

"Why?"

"You give them to me on consignment, and yada, yada, yada, we could make a big profit on them."

"Sorry, they're evidence in the murder case," I say.

He nods. "People have been murdered for less. These are the real deal, legit or not."

Before we leave, he asks me if Laurie is ready to trade in her ring for a more expensive one, but I decline, even though he tells me he could give me a good deal.

I give the stones to Hike to take back to Dylan's office. "Tell Dylan they're fakes," I say, and then smile at Harry. "Not that there's anything wrong with that."

The problem with our case at this point is that we don't have one. We certainly have our suspicions about the Caruso murder being inextricably tied to the Downey killing, but that is just a theory based on Zoe being involved in both. It is not something that would convince a jury; it's unlikely we could even get it admitted to present to a jury.

We have been focusing mostly on the Brantley connection because the Downey case is a relatively simple one, and one that the jury will clearly be able to follow.

Our ability to defend Tommy, independent of Brantley, is very limited. The facts are the facts, and the evidence against our client is very incriminating. There is no alibi; he claims he was at home at the time of the murder, but has no way to prove it.

Tommy had a motive, and there is substantial physical evidence against him. We'll certainly challenge it, but we'll be playing defense the entire time. And the irony of criminal trials is that when the defense plays defense, it loses.

I've been trying to meet with Tommy each day at the jail, though the meetings are brief, and he has no way to be helpful. If he is telling the truth, then by definition there is no chance he has knowledge about what really happened in that house. Rather, he was an innocent nonbystander who was brought into it by events out of his control.

So my visits are not to ask questions and gain insight, but more to let him know that we are working on his behalf, that he is not alone. I could send Hike down to see him, but I'm afraid that after thirty minutes of talking with Hike, he'll hang himself in his cell.

The diamond connection strikes me as important, maybe even crucial. Downey was not the type to have valuable diamonds, especially uncut ones. He did not get them by knocking over a liquor store, or for that matter a local jewelry store.

I also have to assume that whoever killed him was not aware that the diamonds were in the house. According to Pete they were not well hidden; they were simply lying in his dresser drawer. Maybe our arrival on the scene caused the killer to panic and run, but I would have thought he'd make some effort to find the diamonds if he knew they were there. He certainly could have used his knife to compel Downey to reveal their location.

But Downey had the diamonds, and my working theory is that he received them as payment for services rendered. But what were the services?

Stealing Zoe? That would mean he probably got them from Brantley. But then, where would Brantley have gotten them?

Killing Michael Caruso? That would mean he got them from whoever wanted Caruso dead, be it Brantley or someone else. But there is nothing in his record to indicate Downey was a murderer.

So the key is Brantley, with the diamonds the wild card. That is nothing new; they have occupied those positions since the case began. I'm just unfortunately no closer to knowing what part they play.

So if the trial were to start tomorrow, it would be short and ugly. We'd cause Dylan some aggravation, but he would basically roll over us.

Fortunately the trial is not tomorrow; it just feels like it is.

Robby Divine didn't like my asking if he knew anything about diamonds. "Are they worth money?" he asked.

"A lot of money."

"Then I know a lot about them," he said. "Here's a general rule: the more money that is involved, the more I know about it. You haven't picked up on that yet?"

I think Robby may be starting to regret he ever met me at that charity event, since I am constantly asking him for favors. "My friend Harry the jeweler says that Alan Divac is the guy to talk to if I want to learn about importing diamonds," I said. "Do you know him?"

"I should. I own five percent of his company, which I would sell to you, if you were rich."

Robby thinks that the thirty million dollars or so that I have qualifies me for food stamps. "Can you get me in to see him?"

"What am I, your social secretary?"

"That position is currently unfilled. If you're interested in it, I can set up an interview."

Robby declined that offer, but did set up a meeting for me with Alan Divac. His office is on West Forty-seventh Street, not far from the Diamond Exchange. It's raining today, so I allowed for an extra hour to get into the city. I'm not sure why water slows down traffic so much; since cars on these streets never go more than five miles an hour anyway, skidding on the wet pavement seems unlikely.

It's a small office; I only count nine employees on the premises. One of them comes out to greet me, introducing himself as Paul Turner. "Alan is tied up for a while; you can come wait in my office."

I follow him back there, and he offers me something to drink. I take a Diet Coke and sit on the only available chair in his modest office, as he sits behind his desk. "So what did you want to talk to Alan about?" he asks.

"I'll wait for him," I say. "No sense going through it twice."

Turner smiles. "I'm what's commonly called his right-hand man. I'm supposed to find out if I can deal with this without him getting involved."

I return the smile. "I hate to disappoint you."

If he's put off or surprised, he doesn't show it. "No problem. Let's go see Alan."

He takes me down the hall toward a corner office. He opens the door without knocking and brings me into the office, which is considerably larger than Turner's, but by no means impressive. He points to a couch for me to sit on, and takes a chair himself; apparently the right-hand man sits in on meetings.

The man I assume is Alan Divac is on the phone, screaming into it. "What the hell do you think I'm selling you, marbles? Forget it . . . these stones are flawless; you wouldn't know what the hell to do with them." With that, he slams down the phone.

"Wrong number?" I ask.

He laughs. "You can say that again. Robby said you want to learn about diamonds?"

"I do, and—"

He interrupts me. "They are God's most perfect creation."

This guy has obviously never met Laurie and Tara. "I'm interested in the ones that come into the country illegally."

He shoots a quick glance at Turner, probably wondering how I ever got past him. Then he frowns. "Aren't we all. It was the scourge of the business, until we got it mostly under control."

"How was it brought under control?"

"It's called the Kimberley Process. It requires that all diamonds be certified, so that no illegal diamonds can come in from war zones."

"But some do?"

He nods. "Some do. That's why I said mostly under control."

"So the diamonds are merely currency that is used to buy arms?" I ask.

"They can buy anything, but I believe arms are the primary product."

"What does your company do?"

"We import the legitimate stones, then cut and polish them into various shapes, pearl, oval, etc. Once this is done we classify them by the four Cs: cut, color, clarity, and carat weight. Then we sell them to wholesalers or diamond jewelry manufacturers."

"And then it's marked up a thousand percent and sold to dopes like me," I say.

Divac smiles. "Think of it as an extraordinarily beautiful investment." Turner laughs at the comment, though I suspect he's heard Divac say it a thousand times.

I ask Divac if he's heard of Eric Brantley, and he says that he has. I ask, "Could Brantley have been involved in smuggling diamonds?"

He shrugs. "Certainly possible, at least on a small level. You don't need a license to do it; you just have to make the right contacts. But it's a dangerous business to get into, as he may have found out."

"So illegal smugglers would not have appreciated the competition?"

He smiles. "Why would they? The market is finite."

"I want to talk to some people in that world; it's important that I understand them."

"Why?"

"Because I have to have a road map," I say. "These people have committed a murder, and my client is going to trial for it."

"Mr. Carpenter, neither Tommy Infante nor Gerald Downey inhabited the world you are talking about. And if they did, their involvement would have been insignificant."

"You seem to know a lot about them."

Divac and Turner make eye contact. "I have thorough people in my employ." It's clear that Turner has done some research and briefed his boss on me and my case.

"Well, someone thought Gerald Downey was significant enough to slit his throat, and it wasn't Tommy Infante."

"Mr. Carpenter, I understand your obligation to your client. But these are dangerous people, and they have no qualms about killing. For some of them, killing is the only thing they know. They will not let you enter their world and survive."

He says it without much emotion, but it shakes me up a bit. It feels almost like a threat, even if he wouldn't be the person to carry it out. "You trying to cheer me up?"

He smiles, but it is without humor. "I'm trying to save your life."

If it's a saying, then it's wrong: a watched cell phone *does* ring. Stephanie Manning had been watching one for days on end, from the moment she received it in the FedEx package. And finally it rang, so loudly that it seemed shocking in the quiet apartment, but actually no more loudly than any other cell phone. It just seemed deafening to her.

It wasn't a smartphone, just a cell phone, and Stephanie had actually gone online to make sure she knew how to operate it. In her nervousness she didn't want to press the wrong button and accidentally disconnect a call.

So Stephanie pressed the right button, put the phone to her ear, and said "Hello?" She hoped and expected, and even prayed, that she would hear Eric's voice on the other end.

And she did. "Stephanie, it's me."

"Eric, thank God. How are you?"

"I'm doing okay. Steph, I know you don't know what's going on, and you're worried, but everything is going to work out. You need to believe me. But I need your help."

She had a million questions she wanted to ask, but she wanted to give him the room to volunteer information. So she settled on, "What can I do?"

"I need some money."

"I'll give you whatever I have," she said.

"Do you know where Zoe is? I saw her picture online in that newspaper."

"I saw her, Eric. I even played with her. She's fine. Andy Carpenter, the lawyer . . . she's with his partner in the rescue foundation."

"Can you bring her to me?" he asked.

"I don't think so. I asked if I could have her, but they were worried that if she was stolen once, somebody might try to do it again. And then she and I would be in danger."

"I was the one who had her stolen," he said. "So there would be no reason to worry. But you can't tell them that."

"I can try to get her," she said. "Maybe since nothing has happened since then, they'd be willing to change their minds."

"Please try. It's so lonely here. Steph, will you come? I can't wait to see you."

She didn't hesitate. "Of course I will. Can I stay?"

"I wish you could, but it's too dangerous. I need some time to figure things out. Have the police talked to you?"

"No."

"Then you should be fine coming here. I don't see how anyone would know to follow you. Just be careful."

"Where am I going?"

He gave her an address, and she repeated it to him as she wrote it down, since she didn't want to take a chance on getting it wrong. What she didn't realize was that Eric was not the only one she was repeating it for.

Healy had done his homework. He had learned about the relationship between Eric and Stephanie, and figured he might try to reach her. So he had broken into her house and placed three very simple devices in various places inside. From that moment on he had heard everything that was said, which until then wasn't very much.

There had been no downside to placing the devices; in the unlikely event that she found them, no one could ever trace them back to him. The potential upside to doing so was great, and it had just paid huge dividends.

"I'll see you soon," said Stephanie.

Healy smiled. He'd see Eric even sooner.

There are many terrible people in this world. Sometimes it feels like they are everywhere . . . terrorists, murderers, Dallas Cowboy fans . . . but the one really evil group of people who get by relatively undetected are the slimeballs who make children's toys.

Now, I don't want to paint all the toymakers with the same brush; the only truly despicable ones are those that make the toys that have to be assembled. And I especially hate those who put "minimal assembly required" on the outside of the package.

There is no such thing as "minimal assembly." There is "assembly," and there is "no assembly." That's it, no other choices, and I am here to tell you that "assembly" in any form is a vile, disgusting thing.

First of all, they don't use written directions anymore; instead they show pictures, diagrams, drawings. They are absolutely impossible to follow. If NASA used diagrams like this, Neil Armstrong would have gotten out of the capsule and taken one small step onto Connecticut.

The few words they do use to explain the stupid diagrams are in twelve different languages, none of them English. And the one they claim is English is a distortion of the language that cannot be understood by me or any other English-speaking person.

Then comes the most diabolical aspect of the entire process: they always leave out a piece. Every. Single. Time. Sometimes they leave out two or three pieces. I don't know why they do it; it's probably some revenge thing from when they were children themselves.

As hard to believe as it might sound, today I am putting together a parking garage. I have no idea why Ricky wanted it, but Laurie bought it for him, and it's almost as big as an actual parking garage. She either didn't see the "assembly required" tag on the box, or more likely was unconcerned by it.

Right now it looks like a parking garage in Syria that just had air strikes called in on it, as it is in about four hundred pieces all over the room. And yes, there are pieces missing; at least four by my last count. Of course, if I could read French or Chinese, I'd be sure.

What I need now is an interruption, someone or something to get me the hell out of this room. Mercifully, it comes in the form of a ringing doorbell. Moments later Laurie comes into the room and says, "Stephanie Manning is here; she wants to talk to you."

I stand up. "Damn, I was just about to put the finishing touches on this thing."

Laurie looks at the pieces strewn all over the room. "Yeah, it's really coming together."

I go out to the den, where Stephanie is waiting for me. "Hello, Mr. Carpenter, I—"

"Andy."

She nods. "Andy. I know I should have called first, but I'm really anxious, and I thought it would be okay if I came over."

"It's fine, Stephanie. What can I do for you?"

"I've been thinking about it . . . and I'd like to take Zoe home."

"Why?"

"She loves me, and I think she misses Eric. I think being with me will make her happier."

"We talked about this, and you agreed it could be dangerous."

She nods. "I know, but nothing has happened since, right? I'll be careful, and if there's anything unusual, I'll tell you right away. I promise."

My instincts are to once again refuse her request, but I'm reconsidering on the fly. "Have you heard from Eric?" I ask, wanting to see if she'll tell me about the FedEx package.

She shakes her head and lies through her teeth. "No." Then, "Having Zoe around will make me feel like I have a piece of him with me."

I pretend to think about it, but my mind is already made up. "Okay. I'll set it up."

The look of surprise and relief on her face is palpable. "Thank you, Mr. . . . Andy."

We arrange for her to pick up Zoe tomorrow here at the house; I'll ask Willie to bring her over in the morning. She thanks me again and leaves.

Once she's gone, I go back into Ricky's room. Laurie is on the floor with the parking garage, which now looks exactly like a parking garage. "I was just about to finish that," I say.

She nods. "I know. I saw that."

"Did you find the missing pieces?"

"There were no missing pieces."

I nod. "Just as I suspected."

Now that the parking garage issue has been settled, I tell Laurie about my conversation with Stephanie, and my agreement to let her take care of Zoe.

"I thought you were concerned that somebody might come after Zoe again," she says.

"I was, but no one has, and I don't think anyone will. I think it was Eric who sent Downey to take her."

"Why won't he send someone else to try again?"

"I think he has; I'm pretty sure he sent Stephanie here today. Her attitude about it was totally different. The other day she thought it was right that Zoe stay with Willie; now she seemed almost desperate to get her. I think Eric contacted her and put her up to it."

"So Stephanie and Zoe will lead you to Eric?" she asks.

"I think so."

"And if you're wrong, and somebody else is after that dog, for whatever reason? Won't Stephanie and Zoe be in danger?"

"No. We've got Marcus watching her, so now he'll be watching them. No one is in danger when Marcus is on the case."

"So Marcus is going to follow them?"

I nod. "Me and Marcus. Me and Marcus can handle anything."

Professor Charles Horowitz was tired of being scared. He'd been living in a perpetual state of fear ever since Michael Caruso had been killed, and it had only gotten worse when Eric Brantley went on the run.

Actually, if he were to be honest with himself, he would admit that he had been afraid ever since Brantley came to him with the idea. At first he hadn't taken it seriously, hadn't thought that Brantley and Caruso could pull it off. But then, when it took shape and became real, he had encouraged them, even prodded them, to pursue it. And he had enthusiastically signed on as their partner.

Horowitz was an introspective person, and could detach himself enough to be amazed at how the prospect of wealth had changed all of them. They were academics, which by definition meant that they had never pursued the big payoff. But this was going to be so large that they got caught up in it, and never looked back.

Until it was too late.

Horowitz was sure they knew about him, knew that he was part of it. Brantley said that he told them that. He said they were all going to be partners, and they should know who their partners were.

He wasn't sure what happened to destroy the arrangement, what Caruso and Brantley had said or done to result in the disaster it had become. They must have done something to make themselves seem like a threat.

Horowitz didn't want to go to the authorities; that would just result in his own imprisonment. He was out of his league with this, but sensed that his only chance would be to make the people they were dealing with understand that he was not a threat at all, but rather that he was willing to keep his end of the bargain.

So he had contacted them, leaving a message in the manner that Brantley had once described. He felt uncomfortable doing so, not wanting to say anything incriminating into a tape that could then be used to cause his undoing.

He wrote out what he was going to say, and then read it into their machine. He said that he did not want to cause anyone any trouble, that he merely wanted to deliver on the promise that he and "his partner" had made.

The truth was that he really wanted out, that no money was worth the fear he felt. But he believed they wouldn't accept that, and might see him as a continuing threat. So he was willing to go along, because it was essentially the only card he had to play.

And then he waited. And waited some more.

But there was nothing. Not a word. He almost saw it as comical; perhaps he had called a wrong number, and left the message on some old lady's voice mail. Since then she's been playing it for her friends, and they've all been wondering what it could mean.

But, of course, very little about this was comical for Horowitz. Not provoking any reaction was incredibly disconcerting. Did it mean they accepted his terms? And if they hadn't accepted the terms, why had they not come after him?

He didn't know that world, had no idea how they operated. Maybe this was standard operating procedure, or maybe they were out of the country, and hadn't even heard the message. Or maybe they had washed their hands of him, and had moved on. That would be the ideal situation, but Horowitz had no way of knowing if it was fact.

So for the time being, he led a very careful life, only going to work and then going straight home. But the fear was ever present; he likened it to soldiers walking on a trail, knowing a sniper could be out there. Or perhaps they might step on and detonate an IED. They could die in an instant, without ever realizing it. Every moment could be their last.

That was his fear, and one evening when he arrived home, he knew in an instant that it was warranted. He opened his front door, and there in front of him was the scariest human being he had ever seen.

"Hello, Professor. My name is Alek."

They had gotten his message.

Laurie calls Marcus to update him on what is happening. She tells him that it isn't necessary to follow Stephanie when she is not with Zoe, because if she is going to meet up with Eric, there's little doubt that she will take the dog with her. We are not worried about losing her, because Marcus has slipped a small GPS device inside the fender of her car.

Laurie's instructions for him are to contact her when Stephanie is on the move, so that I can join in following her. If we are going to find Eric, then I am going to be the one to talk with him.

Of course, if she flies wherever she is going, then we'll have to improvise. But we'll have a good advance idea if that is going to happen, because she would be taking an airline crate with her to house Zoe. My guess is that she will drive, especially if Eric is in Maine, where the FedEx package came from.

Eric is not a target of mine, unless it turns out that he killed Downey. My goal in this is purely to defend my client; whatever else is going on in Eric's life is not my problem, though it could present me with a moral, if not legal, dilemma.

Eric is a fugitive, charged with the murder of his partner and friend Michael Caruso. If I learn of his whereabouts, I have no affirmative obligation to report it to the police, either as an attorney or a private citizen. But if I truly believe that a murderer is on the loose, then I would morally have to tell the authorities where he is. Other people could conceivably be in danger.

I'll deal with that when the time comes. Circumstances will dictate my actions. It is hard to picture not alerting the authorities to Eric's whereabouts, but right now that is not my concern; I am focused on learning whatever I can to help me defend Tommy Infante.

I walk Ricky, Tara, and Sebastian to school, and when I get back, Willie has arrived with Zoe. She, Tara, and Sebastian do the obligatory sniffing, and all seems fine between them. Tara appears unimpressed, with a look on her face that says, "Another one? You're pushing it, Carpenter." I'm sure I'll hear about this later.

I look out the window and see Stephanie pull up in her car. As we planned, Laurie goes out to greet her at the car and bring her inside. We leave her in the den with Willie and Zoe, while Laurie and I go into the kitchen to make coffee.

"There's a suitcase in her car," she says.

"What about an airline crate?"

She shakes her head. "No." Then, "I'll call Marcus."

The presence of the suitcase indicates a strong likelihood that Stephanie will be bringing Zoe directly to Eric, though it's not a slam dunk that it will happen. But it seems worth it to have me meet up with Marcus right away to do whatever following is necessary.

"I wish I could go with you," Laurie says, knowing she can't do so because of the need to be home with Ricky.

"We could turn it into a family vacation," I say. "A trip to

Maine to talk to a possible murderer. It'll give him something to tell his friends about."

She smiles. "Maybe he can bring the murder weapon to show-and-tell."

We go back into the room to talk to Stephanie. There is no reason to drag this out: I'm sure Marcus is here already, doing the invisible Marcus routine outside. When we walk into the room, Stephanie checks her watch. I would bet anything she is heading straight from here to meet Eric, although based on my level of success betting sports, she's probably going to the dentist.

"Be really careful and alert," I say. "And follow your instincts. If you have any cause for concern, any at all, call me."

"I will," she says. "But we'll be fine. It will be so good to have Zoe with me."

"Are you taking her straight home now?"

She hesitates, and then says, "Yes."

Willie looks unhappy throughout this whole process, and I realize that we haven't had a chance to tell him what is going on. Once Stephanie leaves, I bring him up to date, but it doesn't seem to go over that well. "You're using Zoe as bait?" he asks.

In a way I am, and that has bothered me, but I truly don't think she is in any danger, and I tell him so. "I'll tell Marcus to make Zoe his top priority."

That seems to pacify him some, but I don't have time to discuss it. Marcus is in a car out front, waiting for me to join him. If all goes according to plan, Marcus and I are going to be driving to Maine.

It's fair to say that I am not relishing the idea of seven hours of "alone time" with Marcus.

Eric Brantley didn't know much about being a fugitive. But he did sense that one of the first things they would teach in fugitive school would be not to fall into a pattern, or become predictable. Yet Eric had, in fact, fallen into a pattern. It was a way to keep himself sane and thinking clearly.

Every morning he walked from his house off Route 129 in Walpole, Maine, down to Hanley's Market. He bought whatever supplies he needed there, and even though it was one of those small combination gas station/markets, the food was surprisingly good. They even had pizza that was halfway up to New York standards.

On the way back he always stopped at the Walpole Barn, which sells oysters from the local river, wine, and an assortment of unique gift items that their slogan says are "products for a good life." Eric knew all too well that no one had invented a product that could turn his life around.

Eric frequently bought wine and oysters, and he planned to buy a lot more of them once Stephanie replenished his dwindling money supply. The irony was that he had access to a fortune in diamonds, but no way to turn them into cash he could use. It was frustrating, but not nearly the worst part of his predicament.

The owner of the Walpole Barn was a man named Warren Storch, who seemed to be a friend of everyone in the community. Eric enjoyed his company; it was pretty much the only human contact he had. But of course he could not tell him anything about who he was or why he was there, so it made the conversations fairly one-sided.

Eric took a chance the first time he met Warren. Warren was renting storage space in a second barn he had in the back, and Eric took the space. He brought the materials under cover of darkness and locked them up; Warren could have absolutely no idea how incredibly valuable the items in his barn were.

The round-trip walk, including stops, was about an hour and a half, and it was the highlight of Eric's day. He spent the rest of each day watching television and surfing the web, looking for news stories that might relate to the police search for him, or the major incident that was going to happen miles down the road.

But today was the day Stephanie would arrive with Zoe, so this day was going to be different.

And in fact it was very, very different.

Eric got home and put the groceries and wine on the kitchen table. He was about to unload it when the voice behind him said, "Hello, Eric."

Eric turned, but not to find out who the speaker was. That voice was indelibly planted in his brain. It was the voice of the man who had killed Michael Caruso, and was now going to kill him.

He was surprised to see that Healy was not holding a gun, and had simply pulled up a kitchen chair and sat down. "It's been a while," Healy said.

Even in his fear, Eric sneered. "Yeah, I haven't seen you since you shot Michael in the head."

Healy shrugged. "Had to be done to show we're serious. He wasn't anxious to cooperate."

"And you think I am?"

"I think you want to live. And I think you want your girl-friend to live." Then Healy smiled. "And your dog as well."

"What exactly do you want?" Eric asked.

Healy smiled again. "Very simple, Eric. It's what I've wanted all along. I want us both to make a whole shitload of money."

This is not the first time I've been stuck in a car with Marcus. One time we were actually on a stakeout together, and I found myself hoping that our target would show up and shoot me. Conversationally, it's like being alone, but not nearly as good as actually being alone. Marcus simply does not say anything, and I can't tell what he's thinking. Or if he's thinking.

I learned last time that Marcus listens to classical music, and this time we again agree to share the radio. I get it for an hour; he gets it for an hour. I opt to devote my time to sports talk radio, since I'm obviously an intellectual.

I don't know what it is that he listens to; just a bunch of stuff without words. Classical music is not really my thing, and I know absolutely nothing about it. If you told me you saw Brendel play Brahms last night, I would ask you who won.

We follow Stephanie at a distance, but it's immediately clear when she gets on 95 North that we were correct in our assumption that she's heading to see Eric. We can get closer as she gets farther north, but Marcus is not afraid of losing her, and since I'm afraid of Marcus, I don't question his strategy.

Stephanie stops twice along the way, once in Connecticut and once in New Hampshire. At each stop she walks Zoe, and then pulls into the drive-through at a fast-food restaurant. She obviously doesn't feel comfortable leaving Zoe alone in the car, which wins her points in my book.

We stop once ourselves, to get something to eat and use the restroom. Marcus orders seven double quarter pounders at McDonald's, and proceeds to devour them in an instant, while I drive. One minute they are there, and the next minute they are not. If it wasn't for the fact that I didn't feel a rush of air in the car, I would think he must have thrown them out the window.

We reach New Hampshire, and it feels like just moments later that we're in Maine. There's still another two hours to go until we reach Walpole, which, in terms of car time spent with Marcus, will feel like two weeks.

We get off the highway in Brunswick, and then go through a series of towns along the coast. We enter Wiscasset, which immodestly has a sign proclaiming it the prettiest town in America. I'm not prepared to fully buy into that, although I will admit it's prettier than Paterson.

We go through an even prettier town called Damariscotta, which is only a few minutes from Walpole. Marcus seems to perk up a bit, and gets closer to Stephanie. He clearly has no intention of losing her now.

We make a right turn on Route 29, and the sign says that we are in Walpole. Marcus keeps at a distance but we have Stephanie's car in sight, as she goes another mile before making a left turn. Then she makes a right turn onto a dirt road, which our GPS shows is less than a quarter of a mile long. Marcus stops without turning onto that road, shuts the car off, and opens his door. I sense it's time to get out.

Marcus starts walking up the road, stopping every half minute or so to listen, although what the hell he is listening for I have no idea. I'm walking about five feet behind him, but I can't say that I feel comfortable. I would feel better if I stayed in the car. I would feel even better than that if I had stayed in New Jersey.

We can see a small house in the distance, and Marcus has moved to the side of the road, where we are shielded by trees. We walk a little farther until the silence is pierced by a horrible shriek; I think it's a woman's voice, but I can't be sure. What I can be sure of is that the owner of that voice is in some kind of agony.

Marcus takes off at a full run toward the house, and I do the same. I'm still behind him, but even if I wanted to, I couldn't get anywhere near him. I can now officially add very fast running to the list of Marcus's physical talents.

I can't tell if Marcus has drawn his gun, but I hope he has. Something terrible is going on in that house.

Marcus runs to the front door of the house, and all of a sudden there is no door there. Because I'm behind him, I can't tell if he kicked it down, or if maybe the door saw him coming and fainted in fright. In any event, Marcus is in the house, and I'm in there moments later.

Moments after that I wish I wasn't in there. Everything and everybody is in one room, mainly because the entire ground floor of the house seems to be one open room. There are four humans in the room besides me, but only two of them are living.

The other two, both male adults, are lying facedown on the floor, each in their own pool of blood. The backs of their heads seem to have exploded, no doubt caused by bullets.

Stephanie is shaking and sobbing, and Zoe is sniffing at one of the bodies. I suspect it is Eric, but I certainly can't be sure, and I have absolutely no idea who the other victim is.

I go over to Stephanie and put my arm around her, and then

I lead her outside. There is no sense in my even trying to stop her from crying; what she has just seen would devastate anyone.

Once we're outside, I call 911 and report what has happened. My next two calls are to Pete, to give him a heads-up and tell him that he may need to vouch for Marcus and me, and then to Laurie, just because I want to hear her voice.

I'm getting a little tired of seeing dead people.

Officers from the Lincoln County Sheriff's Department arrive on the scene within three or four minutes, and cars keep pouring in. Based on the number of officers who show up, half the people in Lincoln County must be on the force.

I identify myself to the man who appears to be the lead detective, and miracle of miracles, he's familiar with me because of high-profile cases I've handled, and TV appearances I've made. And even though I'm a defense attorney, he doesn't seem to hate me.

They take us all back to the station house to question us and sort things out. On the way there, just a few minutes from the murder scene, we pass some kind of retail store called the Walpole Barn. There are four police cars in the parking lot.

"What happened there?" I ask the officer driving us.

"They had a break-in," he says.

"You have a lot of crime here? I thought small towns were supposed to be crime-free."

"Not today."

Once we're at the station we begin a process I've become all too familiar with, and one that goes on endlessly. The only positive is that they let us bring Zoe with us, and she gets put in a holding cell while the questioning takes place.

I don't hold anything back in my responses; there's nothing I have to say that can hurt my client. We're all questioned separately, and I pity the cop who drew the short straw and is having to question Marcus.

I ask the detectives the identity of the other victim in Eric's house, but if they know, they clearly have no intention of telling me.

I'm finding myself feeling protective of Stephanie, though I'm not sure why. The only reason we are here is that she lied to me about going to see Eric, and just the act of doing that was aiding and abetting a fugitive. These are not actions that I usually find endearing.

We don't get out of the police station until seven-thirty in the evening, and there is no way any of us are going to drive back to New Jersey tonight. I get us three rooms at a place called Damariscotta Lake Farm in Jefferson because it has a nice restaurant, and I'm starved.

I drive there with Stephanie, me behind the wheel and her sitting in the passenger seat, sobbing. She doesn't want to eat anything, and goes directly to her room. Marcus and I go into the restaurant, and he goes on an eating binge that has to be seen to be believed.

My plan is to drive Stephanie back to New Jersey in her car in the morning, leaving Marcus alone with Mozart. It's been a long day, but I set the alarm for eight o'clock, because I want to get a fairly early start.

Tomorrow is not going to be fun, but it's gotta be better than today.

Compared to this, the drive with Marcus is a laugh riot. We go slightly out of our way and make a quick stop at a place called the Walpole Barn. It was where I saw the four police cars when we went to the police station from the scene of the murder. It seems unlikely that a small town like this would have two large, police-related events that were so close to each other at the same time, without those events being connected.

I suggest that Stephanie wait in the car with Zoe as I go in. The owner, a man named Warren Storch, greets me and seems eager to share what happened. "I was renting storage space to a guy that was new in town, back there in that smaller barn." He points in a direction behind where we were standing.

"What was the guy's name?"

"He told me his name was Walter, but he paid in cash, so I can't say for sure that was really his name, not after what happened. Anyway, he got himself killed yesterday, right up the road from here. And around the same time, somebody broke into that barn."

"Did you see the thief?"

He shakes his head. "No, but they cleaned the place out."

"What had been in there?" I ask.

"I don't know; it wasn't any of my business. I gave him a key, and he kept the place locked. Then yesterday the door was wide open, and it was empty."

He has little more to offer, so I get back into the car and we're on our way. Stephanie has barely said a word, and we've been driving for almost three hours. I've kept the radio off; even though I'd like to hear news reports about the shootings, I'm afraid of the effect it would have on her.

My second choice would be to listen to sports talk radio, but I don't turn that on either. The woman has just experienced a devastating shock and is in mourning; I don't think she cares whether the Giants should draft a running back or an offensive lineman.

Zoe is in the backseat, sleeping. Occasionally she wakes up, looks out the window, and then goes back to sleep. The trip must be going fast for her; I wish she and I could change places.

We stop to walk Zoe at a rest area. I take her on the leash and am surprised when Stephanie gets out of the car and walks alongside us. We walk about twenty feet, and then she says, "He hadn't been the same for a while."

I obviously know she is talking about Eric, so I just ask, "How so?"

"Something was on his mind, driving him. There was always something with Eric; usually it was work, but it could have been anything. He'd get into a topic, and it would consume him. It would be all he would talk about."

"And that changed?"

She shakes her head. "No, I don't think so. But the difference was that this time he didn't talk about it. He kept it from me; I think he kept it from everyone, except maybe Michael."

"You have no idea what it was?" I ask.

"No," she says, then is silent for a while. It's not until we're turning back toward the car that she says, "I think it was about money."

"What do you mean?"

"Money was never really important to Eric; he could have made much more working in private industry. He wanted to be where he could do the best work."

"And that changed?"

She nods. "One day he said to me, 'What would you do if you won the lottery?'"

"A lot of people ask that question."

"Not Eric," she says. "I was surprised he even knew there was a lottery. You'd have to know him to understand, but the question came completely out of left field. And there were others. Once he asked me where I would live if I could live anywhere in the world. These were just not the kind of things Eric ever talked about before."

"How long ago did this start?"

"Maybe a year. I think I noticed it for the first time after he came back from one of those conferences he was always going to."

I ask her where the conference might have been, or what it was about, but she has no idea. To her they were boring scientific meetings, and she wouldn't have gone to one if her life depended on it.

The second half of the trip home is the exact opposite of the first. Whereas she wouldn't talk before, now she can't seem to stop. It's probably cathartic for her, so I just listen. I'm not above pumping her for information that could help my client, but I just don't think she has any.

"I'm sorry I lied to you," she says. "I just wanted to help Eric, and I knew he didn't kill anyone. Do you think people will realize that now?"

"I do," I say, which is the truth. The logical conclusion is that the same person that killed Michael Caruso killed Eric. It isn't necessarily true, but that will be the best guess.

"Do you think I somehow did something that led them to him?"

"I don't," I say, which is not the truth. I think his contacting her and asking her to come up there may well have in some way revealed his location, but I don't know how. "What was in the FedEx package?" I ask.

"You knew about that? It was from Eric, a cell phone, the one he called me on."

She gets quiet for a while, then, "Eric told me he paid someone to take Zoe from you."

I'm not surprised by this, but glad to have it confirmed. "Did he say why?"

"He loved her, and he missed her. Don't you think that's reason enough?" she asks.

"I do."

"What's going to happen to her?"

"What would you like to happen?" I ask.

"I would love for her to be my dog."

I've been thinking about this for a while. Our goal is to find good homes for dogs with people who will love them. If Zoe went to Stephanie's, it would be a good home where she is already loved. "I think that can be arranged, if you really want her," I say.

Stephanie starts to cry, so I'll take that as a yes.

I drop off Stephanie and Zoe at Stephanie's house, and then drive home. As soon as she is out of the car, I turn the radio on. They are not yet reporting the name of the other victim, nor whether the police have any suspects. The only piece of information they are revealing is the one I was dreading, the fact that I was at the murder scene.

Knowing this, I'm not surprised that there is a media mob scene in front of my house when I pull up. I actually have trouble opening the car door because of the throng that surrounds my car, and they fire questions at me as I make my way toward the house.

It's hard to hear everything they are saying, but the gist is that they want to know what I was doing in Maine, and if I have any idea who killed Eric Brantley. I just keep saying no comment, until I'm nearing my front porch, at which point I come to my senses.

None of these people have asked me about the Infante case, because they have no reason to make the connection. Here I have this golden opportunity to enlighten them, as well as the prospective jury pool out there, and I almost blew it. I have definitely lost a foot off my legal fastball.

I stand on my front porch and hold my hands up, asking for

quiet. It's sort of an impromptu press conference situation, as I am standing on the top steps and the media is in front of and below me. I am above the masses and they are hanging on my every word; I feel like I should sing "Don't Cry for Me Argentina."

"I don't have too much to say" is how I begin. "It's been a long couple of days, and there's a lot I can't say about it. But I do want everyone to understand that what happened in Maine yesterday was a terrible tragedy. My condolences and thoughts go to the victims and their families.

"There is obviously a lot of confusion surrounding these events, but one thing is absolutely clear. Tommy Infante sits in jail, wrongfully accused of murder. My hope is that the prosecutor, Mr. Campbell, will not be the last one to realize this. Thank you."

As I finish, there is a moment of strange silence. I can see in their faces that they want to throw out questions, but they are trying to process what Tommy Infante possibly could have to do with the murders in Maine.

It's all I can do not to laugh as I turn and go into the house. I'm no sooner in the door than Ricky comes running up to me, with Laurie behind him.

"Dad! I just saw you on television! You were in front of our house!"

"I know, Rick."

"Why were you on?"

"It was for my job," I say.

"Cool! I want to do that job when I get big. Can I?"

"Sure. You can go to law school in the offseason. Spring training doesn't start until February."

Satisfied with the outcome of the conversation, Ricky turns to Laurie. "Hey, Mom! Dad says I can go to law school before spring something!"

"That's wonderful, Rick."

"I'm going to be on television!"

Ricky runs out of the room, probably to start filling out his law school applications. That leaves Laurie and I alone, so we can talk about shootings and murders and robberies, the things that she and I can romantically share.

"You doing okay?" she asks. "You've been having a rough time lately."

I nod. "It's pretty hard to get used to. It was an ugly scene, and for Stephanie to walk in on it . . ."

"You said they were executed? Shot in the back of the head?"

"That's what it looked like to me. I didn't hang around in there much."

She looks puzzled. "They just ran a report on CNN . . . you might want to turn it on."

I walk over and turn the television on to CNN, and it has a huge BREAKING NEWS banner plastered across the bottom of the screen. It's part of the trend in television news, everything is treated as a monumental revelation worthy of being declared BREAKING NEWS. I'm waiting for the time when they announce the BREAKING NEWS that there is no BREAKING NEWS.

It's what's under the banner that gets my attention. It says, "FBI: Brantley Death is Murder-Suicide." There is no way that can be the case, unless one of the victims shot the other, then lay facedown, reached around, and shot himself in the head. Then, remarkably, his dead body would have had to discard the gun, since I didn't see any weapon near the bodies.

"This is crap," I say, since I am nothing if not eloquent.

Laurie nods. "That's what I thought you'd say. You were under a lot of stress; is it possible you saw it wrong?"

"It is not possible. But you should check with Marcus. He got in the room even before I did, and he is not familiar with the concept of stress."

"So let's assume you remember it correctly. Why would they be giving out false information?"

"The easy answer is there is something they want to conceal, and it must be something significant, because in this day and age it's hard to sell bullshit stories like this. The local cops on the scene know the truth. Marcus, Stephanie, and I know the truth. But the FBI seems to have created their own truth."

As I am saying that, another significant question comes to mind. "And why the hell was the FBI there in the first place? Two guys got murdered in a city in Maine; what about that brings the Bureau in?"

"It's interstate," Laurie says. "Brantley's case goes from New Jersey to Maine."

"Maybe, but the FBI was in on it immediately. They swooped in like they were ready for it; there wasn't time for the locals to have invited them in."

I'm thinking about this like a lawyer, which I guess is sort of appropriate, since that's what I am. But I don't care that much about what it is they're hiding about Eric Brantley; my focus is how I can use my knowledge of the truth as a bargaining chip for Tommy Infante.

"Have they said anything about the other victim?" I ask.

"I don't think so, unless it's been in the last few minutes. I think one of the commentators referred to him as an associate of Brantley's."

I nod. "Getting killed with someone definitely makes him worthy of the associate label."

"So where are you going to take this?" she asks.

"Nowhere. They're going to come to us."

Alan Divac was experiencing a particular feeling for the first time. It was the sense that things were moving out of his control, something that simply did not happen to him. Divac was used to calling the shots, and never, ever being surprised.

The visit from the lawyer, Carpenter, was a little disconcerting, but no big deal. Carpenter was flailing around in the dark, with no real knowledge about what was happening. The fact that he wanted Divac to provide him with a road map to the illegal diamond business was unintentionally comical, but it was not a joke that Divac could share with him.

Divac had believed that Downey's death was unrelated to his own business, and that Carpenter was defending a guilty man. Now he was not so sure. Because now Brantley was dead, and Divac's sources told him that Healy was as well. Divac hadn't ordered the killings, although he certainly was not going to mourn for Brantley. Brantley was a competitor, and though that didn't warrant a death sentence, it wasn't going to keep Divac up nights.

But the fact that it had happened without his knowledge, and more importantly the fact that Healy was another victim, added a new and ominous aspect to the situation. Divac was feeling isolated, and unsure of his next move. He had taken to relying on Healy to help deal with these kinds of situations, but now Healy was gone.

All of this meant that a new player had entered the game, and if that player was able to handle Healy, he was going to be hard to deal with.

As I predicted, it doesn't take long for the FBI to show up. I came down to the office, since that's the most likely place they'd be looking for me. And sure enough, thirty minutes after I get here, two FBI agents come walking through the door.

So my prediction has come to pass, except for the fact that while they look and sound exactly like FBI agents, that's not what they are. They are with Immigration and Customs Enforcement, better known as ICE.

One of them is at least six-three, and the other no more than five-eleven. They are wearing the exact same navy suit, different only in that one of them must have four inches less material. Usually I find that it's the shorter agent who speaks first, though I have no idea why.

Once again my short/tall theory holds, and the shorter one speaks. "I'm Agent Hernandez, and this is Agent Gardiner."

I find it important to demonstrate early on in these conversations that I am not intimidated. "Both of your first names are Agent? Wow, what are the odds against that?"

"I heard you were a pain in the ass," he says.

"How? I've never dealt with ICE before. Are you guys finally communicating between agencies? That's comforting."

They are obviously quick learners, because we are only a few seconds into a conversation, and they've already learned to ignore my bullshit. "What were you doing in Maine yesterday?" Hernandez asks.

"I was white-water rafting. You ever try it? It's quite an adventure."

This time it's Gardiner. "I would suggest you start answering our questions."

"Okay. Hey, wait . . . I've got an even better idea. Let's answer each other's questions; I'll start. Why does ICE care why I was in Maine? And who was the other dead guy in that house besides Eric Brantley? And what was in the storage barn that was broken into? You can answer them in any order you like."

"Carpenter, you are making a mistake."

"No, I am defending my client. If this conversation is not going to benefit Tommy Infante, then there isn't going to be a conversation. So if those terms don't work for you, then get the hell out of here. In which case the only thing you will hear from me is a statement to the media saying that was no murder-suicide in that house."

The two agents look at each other, practicing silent agent-speak, and then they stand up. "We'll be back real soon," Hernandez says.

"Great. It will give me something to look forward to."

They leave, and I'm pleased with how it went. In a perfect world, they would have filled in many of the blanks that I have about Eric Brantley and the murders yesterday, but I had no expectations of that.

The reason I'm pleased is that I accomplished one thing and learned another. I let them know that I am not going to be a pushover; that if they need something from me they are going to have to pay for it in terms of information. They may decide that they can do without me, but at least the ground rules have been set.

I've learned something simply based on the agency for whom they work. It's an Immigration and Customs case, and while I don't know any of the details, just knowing that is a plus. I doubt that Brantley was smuggling immigrants in across the border; a much better guess would be that he was somehow involved in illegal goods.

Diamonds come to mind.

I call Sam, and he answers on the first ring. I don't know how he does it, but he has answered on the first ring every single time I have ever called him. He must have his cell phone taped to his ear.

He answers with "Talk to me." That's how he talks when he's working on a case for me, in crisp clean phrases. I half expect him to say "roger" and "wilco." When we're not on a case, he'll just answer with, "Hey, Andy, what's going on?"

"Hello, Sam."

"Did you really discover those bodies up in Maine?"

"I was one of the people who did, yes."

"How cool is that?" he asks, clearly jealous at my proximity to the action.

"Supercool, Sam. Supercool. I've got a job for you."

"Great. I'm ready."

"I want to know everywhere Eric Brantley traveled in the last two years. I'm most interested in travel abroad, and travel for business conferences, but I want everything."

"Piece of cake."

"Ten-four," I say, before hanging up.

I head down to the jail to see Tommy Infante. I haven't been there in a few days, which I'm feeling guilty about. I like my clients to see my adorable face on a daily basis, so they won't feel so alone.

I'm not sure how much I should tell him about what's been going on, but my decision is made for me by his first question. "What the hell were you doing in Maine?"

Prisoners in the jail have access to some media, and he's obviously seen reports about the Brantley murder and my being on the scene. I'm certainly not going to lie to him about it, so I lay it all out. There doesn't seem to be any potential harm in doing so, since I'm not revealing any inside information or insight. I wish I had some to reveal.

Tommy's stress has seemed to increase of late, which is no surprise. The trial date is approaching, and there is no greater pressure in the world than waiting for a jury to decide your future.

When I'm finished describing the situation in Maine, Tommy asks, "What does Brantley have to do with me? Just the dog?"

"The dog and probably the diamonds."

"And who was the other dead guy?"

"I don't know; they're not releasing his name."

"I'm in pretty deep shit here, aren't I?"

I sometimes don't tell my clients everything, but I never lie to them. "I would say the shit is pretty deep, yes. It's approaching eye level. But we're digging away."

The burden of preparing for the Infante trial has fallen on Hike. That has freed me up for wasting my time and learning nothing whatsoever about unrelated murders that have nothing to do with the case I'm defending.

On the positive side, I have my closing summation already prepared and ready to go. "Ladies and gentlemen of the jury, Tommy Infante is innocent, because the victim stole someone else's dog, and he had some diamonds."

Hike and I are meeting in the office to go over where we stand in trial preparation. It's a big day; even Edna has made an appearance. She explained that she doesn't want to overprepare for the upcoming crossword puzzle tournament, so doing some work might take her mind off it. Gee, I hope it does.

Hike has done his usual professional job of interviewing prospective witnesses and preparing strategies for each of them on the witness stand. "I've got a couple more witnesses to question, but I need some help on it," he says.

"Who are they?"

"Well, in the discovery it mentions that Tommy and the victim knocked over a jewelry store, and part of their motive is that Downey didn't share the take with Tommy. That's what Tommy apparently said when he threatened Downey in the bar. But there's no indication as to which store it was, and no interview with the store owner."

"Okay, I'll find out from Tommy."

"Good," he says. "Last thing: somebody needs to talk to the bartender, a guy named Dan Hendricks, and it ain't going to be me," he says.

He's referring to the bartender on duty at the Market Street bar the night that Tommy threatened to slit Downey's throat, a promise that somebody made good on. "What's the problem?" I ask.

"The people in that particular establishment didn't appreciate what they considered an intrusion. They seemed inclined to physically harm the intruder, who in this case was me."

"They scared you off?" I ask. "Couldn't you go at a time when it was fairly empty?"

He nods. "They did, and I couldn't. This particular bartender only works nights, when it's crowded. Effective immediately, I only work days."

This presents me with a dilemma. Hike is not exactly a Navy SEAL, and he and I occupy a similar ranking on the courage scale. I call Laurie, who hears the situation and says, "I'll get a sitter and go with you tonight."

I have an attitude that I'm afraid it's fair to describe as sexist. If I am going to pathetically cower behind someone for protection, I prefer it to be a man. And if it has to be a woman, I'd like it to be someone other than the mother of my child.

"I was thinking Marcus," I say.

"You don't think I can handle it?" She and I both know that as a former police officer she can handle it quite well.

"I see you more as a delicate flower."

"Okay, I'll call Marcus. It would be tough to get a sitter for tonight anyway."

I tell Laurie to arrange for Marcus to pick me up at home at eight o'clock, which will give me time to join her and Ricky for dinner, and then have a drink to fortify myself. I suspect Hike has been overstating the hostile atmosphere in the bar, but I still could use a little alcoholic reinforcement, in addition to Marcus.

I wind up deciding not to have the drink, since my tolerance for it seems to decrease every year. It must be a thing about getting older or maybe falling out of practice; I used to be able to handle my liquor quite well, but now if I see a beer commercial I get woozy.

Marcus is never late, and he's never early, so I walk outside at 7:59, and as I'm reaching the curb, he pulls up. I get in and say, "How are you, Marcus?" and I think he grunts a greeting, but I can't be sure because the classical music is turned up high.

I gently reach over and turn it down a little, so that he can hear me explain where we're going and why, although I think Laurie has already done so. He doesn't kill me, so I take that as a sign that I can start my explanation.

The bar is called the Study Hall, as incongruous a name as any I have ever heard. It's a few blocks from Eastside High School, which is where I went. In those days it was a luncheonette called the Cozy. We went there every day so that I could have lunch and be rejected by girls.

Then the powers that be decided that students should have to eat lunch at school, which ensured the Cozy's sudden demise. We couldn't go there anymore, which meant I had to bring my own lunch and be rejected by girls on school grounds. The Cozy has reopened as a seedy bar, and the "Study Hall" name must be some backhanded reference to the fact that it is near the school.

My plan is to leave Marcus outside, and only have him come in if I need him. The reason for that is that Marcus can make people a tad uncomfortable, and if the conversation with the bartender can take place with him feeling free and unintimidated, I'm likely to get more out of him.

As they say, war plans change as soon as the enemy is encountered, and my plan changes when we pull up to the bar. The Study Hall is a tough place in a very tough neighborhood, and it's fair to say that very little "studying" takes place here.

I don't even have to tell Marcus about the change in strategy; he simply opens his door and gets out. He has a rather good understanding of my capabilities.

We enter the bar, which is actually not crowded at all. There are maybe a dozen patrons, including two very large men in T-shirts three sizes too small who are playing pool at a table near the bar. Every single person in this bar could kick my ass, including the two women seated at a table next to the jukebox.

I can sense that just about everyone is watching us, though I don't know if it's Marcus or me that is drawing the most attention. As out of place as I look in here, my guess would be Marcus.

I steal a look at my cell phone, to see if there is cell service here in case I have to call 911. I doubt I will, since Marcus is rather reliable, but it can't hurt to be sure. My phone has no bars, so Marcus is on his own.

We go to the bar, which only has two people sitting at it. They're watching the Yankees game on television, as is the bartender. He's leaning on the bar, hand supporting his chin, as he watches.

"You got some customers, Dan." It's one of the people at the bar, being helpful as Dan hasn't seemed to notice our arrival.

Hike said his name was Dan Hendricks, so this is the guy we're looking for.

"Yeah?" he says. I think he's asking us what we want, but he could be just acknowledging what the guy at the bar said. I don't think Hendricks has a future in sales. But he adds, "What are you drinking?"

"Sarsaparilla," I say. "And make it a double." I'm not sure why I say stupid, irritating stuff when people annoy me, or when they don't annoy me, but I've learned to live with it.

"What?" is his appropriate response.

"We just want to ask you some questions."

That makes him alert to the point that he actually stands up. "About Gerald Downey," I add.

"You cops? Because I already spoke to the cops three times."

"No. I'm an attorney representing Tommy Infante."

He sneers. "Another one?" He calls out to the two very large guys playing pool. "Hey, we got another lawyer for the guy who killed Gerry."

"Allegedly killed Gerry," I say. "You need to have more respect for due process."

He doesn't seem to want to debate that technical legal point. Instead he says, "There was some downer guy in here asking questions last week."

"He is my associate." I point to Marcus. "This is my other associate."

"He's your muscle?" Hendricks asks, meaning Marcus, and apparently disrespecting my own muscles.

"Hey, I work out a half hour a week on the treadmill, at a one percent incline. You ready for the questions?"

Before he can answer, I turn and see the two pool players coming toward us. The one in front is still holding his cue stick. I don't think they're going to ask us if we want to play winners.

Cue Stick Man says, "Get the hell out of here."

I nod. "We're actually on the same page on this. This does not seem like an establishment I want to patronize for any length of time. But I do need to get these questions answered."

I look over at Marcus to make sure he is ready to rush to my defense, but if he's tense and ready to pounce, he's hiding it really well. His eyes are half open, which is the only way I know he isn't asleep.

Cue Stick Man and his friend are moving closer, and Cue Stick says, threateningly, "You want some answers, pal?"

"Marcus, you might want to consider getting involved at some point," I say. I get no reaction, so I add, "We might even be approaching that point."

Cue Stick Man says, "Side ball in the corner pocket, shithead," and twists his body to swing the cue stick at me, since I am apparently "shithead," and my head is the ball. I instinctively start to duck, which is a shame, because I don't get a great look at what happens next.

One moment Cue Stick Man is swinging the stick at my head, while Marcus sits there watching. The next moment, Marcus is standing and somehow has stopped and confiscated the stick in one almost imperceptible movement.

Clearly not content to have taken away the stick, Marcus lowers it and then swings it straight up into Cue Stick Man's groin. Since he came to the bar to play pool rather than football, I doubt that Cue Stick Man thought to wear a protective cup. His scream is not one I'm likely to forget soon.

Marcus then hits him in the jaw, not with full Marcus force but enough to cause major damage. He slumps forward and goes straight to the floor. Friend of Cue Stick Man, clearly the smarter of the two, does not seem inclined to intervene, and he backs off. If he's going to shoot any more pool, he'll need a different stick, since his friend is starting to retch and throw up on this one.

I turn to the bartender and say, "Much to your surprise, my associate has prevailed over your associate."

It wasn't part of Alek's makeup to get annoyed. He did what he had to do, professionally and absent emotion. Getting annoyed about it, or stressed about it, or even pleased with it, was a waste of time and energy.

This assignment in the New York area was a perfect example. It had been planned as a simple mission: he was to deal with Brantley, Healy, and Horowitz. The fact that Brantley and Healy had been together made it quicker and easier, but it didn't matter much to Alek either way. From the moment he got the assignment, the two men were doomed.

And that was to be it. Alek even had the complicated documents that he would use on the long trip home, and he was only six hours from his flight time when the new set of instructions came in.

He was to remain in the United States for possible additional assignments. He was to facilitate the entire operation in Maine; there was no one else to do it.

There was also a tentative new target, a lawyer who was apparently conducting an investigation that was a potential danger to Alek's employers. The course of that investigation would determine whether the target would be finalized.

Alek had no desire to stay in the United States, but like everything else, he took it in stride. Whatever he needed to do, he would do, and then he would move on.

Whether or not he killed the lawyer was of no particular consequence to him.

Hendricks seems to have undergone a sudden attitude change. He stares at Marcus, then at the fallen Cue Stick Man, and says to me, "Holy shit, did you see that?"

"Just another day at the office, my friend. Just another day at the office. Now, if we can get these questions out of the way. . . ."

"What? Oh, sure, anything you want to know."

"Was Gerry Downey a regular in here?"

"Gerry? Yeah, sure, five nights a week, maybe six."

"What about Tommy Infante?"

"That the guy that iced him?" he asks.

I once again feel a lawyer's obligation to correct him. "That's the guy who's accused of icing him."

Hendricks nods his agreement; after watching Marcus in action, he would agree if I told him the Knicks were going to win the Super Bowl. "Right," he says. "Absolutely. That guy never came in; that was the first time I had ever seen him."

He goes on to describe the argument. They were sitting at the bar, not doing anything unusual, when suddenly they started yelling. According to Hendricks, Tommy was by far the angrier of the two, screaming profanities at Downey.

"He kept screaming things like, 'You'll die for this, you son of a bitch. I'll slit your goddamn throat!' He must have threatened to slit Gerry's throat three or four times, easy."

"What did Gerry do?" I ask.

"Not much; he kept saying he didn't know what the other guy was talking about. He didn't understand what was going on, but when the other guy wouldn't shut up, Gerry went in the back and made a call to some friends, who came and threw the guy out."

"Who were the friends?"

Hendricks points to Cue Stick Man, still out of it, but moaning slightly. "That's one of them."

"So Downey had a lot of friends here?"

Hendricks nods. "Absolutely. He was one of the guys, one of the regulars."

The way Hendricks says that jars me into thinking about an angle I hadn't thought about before, and one I should have pursued.

I know that Eric Brantley hired Gerry Downey to steal his dog. What I don't know is how Eric Brantley knew Gerry Downey in the first place. Brantley was an academic, living and working in a relatively sheltered environment. Downey was a thief, and not a high-class one at that. One hung out on campus, and one hung out in this dive of a bar in downtown Paterson.

Additionally, Brantley couldn't have known he would need to have his own dog stolen until he was on the run and hiding in small-town Maine. I imagine that would have made finding a dog thief in Paterson that much tougher. You don't find dog thieves advertising in phone books.

So my best guess is that Brantley must have known Gerry Downey before he fled. If I can find out how, it might solve a big part of this puzzle. Or maybe they were second cousins, in which case it will solve nothing.

"Have you read about Eric Brantley?" I ask.

"I don't do much reading," Hendricks says.

"He was wanted for murder, and then he was just found murdered himself, in Maine."

"Oh yeah, sure. I saw the story on television. What about him?"

"Did you ever see him in person?" I ask. "Was he ever in here?"

"They said the guy was like a scientist, or a professor, or something. You think a guy like that would show up in here?"

He's right; even though I never met Eric Brantley, I can't see him hanging out in this dump. But I also can't see him having a connection to Gerry Downey, yet he obviously did.

So many things to figure out, and so little time. . . .

I'm surprised that the customs agents haven't come back to me. It's been four days, and I would have thought by now they would return, either to try and strong-arm me into answering their questions, or to take a more cooperative approach. But neither has happened.

The media has still not come up with an identification of the other victim in the Brantley shooting. He is just said to be an associate of Brantley's, with no other description given. They don't seem to be pressing the matter too hard; the Brantley case has left the front burner.

I've called Pete to see if he can find out anything about him, and he said that he would check with the detectives working on the case.

This morning I'm headed over to Stephanie's. I'd like to say that I'm concerned about her and want to see how she's doing, and while that's true, it's not my primary reason for visiting her.

When I called and asked if I could come over, she sounded down, but said she was back to work. She works out of her house. I like that, because it means Zoe always has companionship.

When I arrive, Stephanie and Zoe are just entering the house, apparently back from a walk. She waves to me, and waits for me to get out of the car, so we go in the house together.

I ask how things are going, and she smiles a little sadly and says, "I'm doing okay. Zoe is a big help; I think we're helping each other."

"I'm glad she's got such a great home," I say, because I am. "I'd like to ask you a question."

She looks wary. "About Eric?"

I shake my head. "Not this time."

I take a photograph out of my pocket, which is of Gerry Downey. "Have you ever seen this person?"

She looks at it and says, "Isn't he the guy who was murdered?"

"Yes."

"I saw his picture on television when it happened."

"You didn't see him prior to that?"

"I don't think so. Why?"

"He's the guy Eric hired to steal Zoe. I'm trying to figure out how they knew each other."

"I wish I could help, but I have no idea."

Her answer disappoints but doesn't surprise me. Clearly Eric Brantley was not into sharing everything in his life with Stephanie; she knows almost as little about him as I do.

I tell Stephanie that I might need her to testify at Tommy's trial. "Whatever you need," she says. "I'm very grateful to you."

Cindy Spodek is an FBI agent and second in command at the Boston office. Our paths crossed on a couple of cases when she was working in New Jersey, and Laurie and I have become friends with her over time.

Of course, Laurie and I have different ways of demonstrating our friendships. For Laurie, it's keeping in touch and seeing Cindy whenever she can, enjoying each other's company, and being involved in each other's lives. For me, it's calling Cindy whenever I can take advantage of her position to give me information or otherwise help me on a case.

I haven't talked to her since the last time I needed her, so I'm surprised when she calls me on my cell on the way home.

"Andy, long time no talk."

"Don't tell me you want something from me again," I say. "I wish our friendship could be based on something deeper."

"Don't be a wiseass, Andy."

"It's involuntary. How are you, Cindy?"

"I'm not happy, and you're the cause of it."

"Let me guess," I say. "You've been asked to call me to help resolve a problem that another governmental agency is having."

"You got it. For some reason next to my name it says, 'When Andy Carpenter is being a pain in the ass, this is who you call.'"

"So knowing me has gotten you a special status?"

"Yeah," she says, and I can almost see her snarling through the phone. "Real special. Andy, you need to talk to these people. This is important."

"The question of whether my client spends the rest of his life in prison is rather important as well."

"What does this have to do with your client?"

"That's what I'm trying to find out."

She sighs audibly. "Okay, previous rules apply?"

"Previous rules apply."

Over time Cindy and I have had a few negotiations like this, and we've always come to the same resolution, so by now we can shorthand it. Each side will tell the other as much as they can without jeopardizing the job they have to do. The government's job is to protect the public and stop crime; my job is to defend my client.

"Good," she says. "Hopefully this will be the last I hear about it."

"One more thing," I say.

"Uh-oh."

"I know you won't tell me what is going on, because it's not your case, but tell me this."

"Uh-oh," she repeats.

"From the government standpoint, are innocent lives at stake?"

She hesitates for a moment, then, "Yes. Definitely."

"Got it. Thanks."

"Does that mean you'll be more cooperative?" she asks.

"No. It means I have more leverage."

I pay another morning visit to Tommy at the jail. Early mornings are the best time for me to do it, since it leaves me the rest of the day to focus on the case. The trial date is barreling down on us, which means that every minute counts.

I don't have much to bring him up to date on, and he is of course disappointed to hear that. He is also still growing increasingly anxious and worried, but there is really nothing I can do about it.

All I can do this visit is ask him a question. "Which jewelry store did you help Downey rob?"

"Why?"

"We need to talk to the owner, so we can be prepared when the prosecution calls him as a witness." The prosecution still hasn't turned over any discovery documents relating to the robbery, but it will help to be prepared when they inevitably get around to it.

He nods his understanding. "It's called Mid-City Jewelers; it's a combination jewelry store–pawn shop."

"I know where it is," I say. It's only about six blocks from my office; I'll be able to stop on the way back. This way the poor owner won't have to talk to Hike. No sense victimizing him twice.

Mid-City Jewelers is located on what is not much more than an alleyway off Market Street. As Tommy said, it is a combination jewelry store—pawn shop, but based on the signs in the window, it seems as if the pawn shop aspect is dominant. Tommy said he drove the getaway car, and parked a little farther down the alley when Downey went inside. It's easy to see how he could have done so unnoticed at the late-night hour the robbery was done.

The store is empty except for a guy who is apparently the proprietor, since he is sitting behind the counter. He looks up at me and says, "Andy Carpenter, what the hell are you doing here?"

I have no idea who he is, so I ask him if we know each other.

"I'm Bill Waldron. I was a witness in a murder trial, the one where that rich guy got shot in the head."

I think I know which case he's talking about, but if I'm right it was probably ten years ago. If Bill Waldron remembers that so vividly, he likely hasn't had that many exciting experiences since then.

"Was I nice to you on the stand?" I ask.

"You were great; questions were easy. I asked for some water, and you gave me time to drink it. It was pretty cool."

I am Andy Carpenter, provider of water to the masses. "Good to hear. I've got a few more questions, this time with no jury present."

"About the same case?"

"No, a new one," I say. "You might be called into court again."

"Great, no problem. Fire away." Then he smiles and says, "If I need water again, I'll just ask for it."

"You had a robbery here a couple of months ago, middle of the night. I want to know—"

He interrupts me. "We didn't have any robbery."

That was not the answer I was expecting. "Are you the owner?"

"Yup. I have one other employee, but he works maybe ten hours a week, when I have something else to do."

"This robbery happened in the middle of the night."

"Well, they didn't set off the alarm, and they didn't take anything. Robberies like that I can live with."

I have no idea if he's telling the truth, but I'm not seeing any sign of stress or evasion. So my keen power of intuition tells me that he's either telling the truth, or lying through his teeth. I press on, "So you never reported a robbery to the police?"

"Why would I? I'm telling you, there was no robbery. We had one about six years ago, but you don't mean that, right?"

"Right. Did you have in your possession two large, uncut diamonds, about three carats each?"

His response is to laugh out loud. "Come on, look at this place."

"Do you check your inventory often?"

"Of course; there's not that much to check. I'm telling you, you must be confusing this with a different store. Nobody broke in here."

I thank him and leave. All I've succeeded in doing is adding to my list of questions.

Why would Downey have Tommy drive him to this store, and claim he robbed the place, if he didn't?

And assuming Downey did commit the robbery, why would the victim be denying it?

When I leave the store, something truly stunning happens. I call my office phone to retrieve messages off voice mail, and Edna answers! She says "Mr. Carpenter's office," just like she's supposed to! The odds of that rank with getting hit by lightning while being attacked by a crocodile on the day the Mets win the World Cup.

"Edna, are you okay?" I ask, knowing full well that if a pod has taken over her body, I won't get a truthful response.

"Yes, I'm fine. There are two gentlemen here to see you, from Immigration and Customs Enforcement."

That explains the good behavior; she's trying to impress the agents. If she knew how, she'd probably make them coffee. "Tell them I'll be there in fifteen minutes."

I'm going to have to handle this carefully. This is supposed to be an exchange of information, but hard information is something I really don't have. I strongly doubt they're going to be fine with a one-way street.

When I arrive, Agents Gardiner and Hernandez are standing near Edna's desk, looking over her shoulder, as she continues her training for the crossword puzzle tournament. "You see? It fits perfectly," she tells them. "You don't fight the puzzle; you take what it gives you."

I'm sure that's wise counsel, but I have no idea what it means. The agents turn when they realize I'm in the room, and Gardiner says, "She's amazing."

"You have no idea," I say. "Let's go in my office."

Once we're in there and have all sat down, Hernandez says, "My hope is that we can do this without any bullshit."

"It springs eternal," I say. "I'll start. The guy that was killed with Brantley, what is his real name?"

"Raymond Healy. But we do not want that name released to the public."

"Who is he?"

"He *was* a diamond smuggler, but he murdered his contact in South Africa, and was temporarily short of product."

"What was he doing with Brantley?" I ask.

"Why don't you tell us?"

"I can only tell you what I think," I say. "Brantley somehow got himself into the diamond business; it's likely he made contacts on one of his trips abroad. I'm getting information on that now. But he hired a guy named Gerry Downey to steal his dog, and Downey had two nearly perfect uncut diamonds in his possession. I can't imagine they came from anyone other than Brantley."

"How did Brantley know Downey?" Hernandez asks.

"I'm working on that now; I'll let you know when I know. Who killed Brantley and Healy?"

Hernandez doesn't answer, and instead takes out a photograph and shows it to me. It's hard to tell how big the man in the photo is, but I can tell that he is not someone I would want to know. Or talk to. Or be on the same planet with. "You know this guy?" he asks.

"No, but he looks like a barrel of laughs. Who is he?"

"He goes by the name of Alek. He's Georgian."

"I assume you mean the country, not the state," I say. "Is he the killer?"

"Probably. He's certainly *a* killer, and we have reason to believe he is in the country. He is as dangerous as anyone you have ever met, or heard about, or seen in the movies."

"What does Georgia have to do with smuggled diamonds? I thought they mostly came from West Africa."

"That's where they start. But they wind up being used as currency to supply illegal arms all over the world. Those arms sometimes kill Americans. Alek and his friends have supplied the weapons that have killed a lot of people."

"So Brantley and Healy died in a dispute over diamonds?" I ask. "Divac warned me that these were dangerous people."

Gardiner seems surprised. "You talked to Alan Divac?"

I nod. "Yes, I wanted to learn more about how diamonds get into this country, and I was told he was the go-to guy. Why?" Clearly Gardiner knows Divac; it seemed to press a button when I mentioned him.

"Just gathering information," Gardiner says. "What were you doing in Maine?"

"I found out Brantley was there, so I was going to try and get some answers."

"To what?"

"I don't believe the Downey murder is separate from all this."

Hernandez shakes his head and interrupts. "Downey's a bit player."

"Maybe so," I say. "But if I can tie his murder in, then my client walks. Simple as that."

"You haven't told us shit," Gardiner says.

I shake my head. "That's overstating it. But as I learn more,

I'll keep you in the loop, as long as it doesn't jeopardize my client. I hope you'll do the same."

Hernandez smiles. "It springs eternal." Then, "Maybe your client is guilty."

"Hopefully you won't be on the jury."

It wasn't until an hour later that I realized what Agent Hernandez said. When I brought up Gerry Downey's name, Hernandez had described him as "a bit player." He didn't say that Downey wasn't involved in the diamond smuggling, nor did he say that Downey's murder wasn't tied in. Instead he was saying that Downey wasn't important. Of course, what's important to the U.S. government isn't necessarily what's important to me and my client.

In any event, dismissing someone as unimportant implies a familiarity with that person. Customs agents wouldn't be familiar with Downey because he knocked over a jewelry store, or even because he got himself murdered, unless he had something to do with a case they were investigating.

Hernandez's comment reinforces the need for me to tie Downey and Brantley together. I know the link exists, because Brantley told Stephanie that he hired someone to steal Zoe, and I know that Downey was the one who committed the theft. But I need to prove it to the jury, and I need to prove that it relates to whatever the hell is going on with the diamonds.

I can go back to Hernandez and press him on it, but I feel like I should wait until I have more information to trade. When

I need crucial information about murder victims, I turn to the obvious people for help: Hilda and Eli Mandlebaum.

Under Sam's supervision, Eli and Hilda, as well as Leon Goldberg and Morris Fishman, have been going over the names on Downey's phone records. It's basically been a fishing expedition, since, as Sam described it, they are just names.

But I've been thinking of Downey as a victim, and while he is certainly that, he is also a "player," bit or otherwise. The more I can learn about him, the greater the chance I can discover why he was killed. That might be the key to understanding who wanted him dead, and obviously got what they wanted.

I call Sam, and he tells me that the team is with him at the office, and they can tell me what they've learned. "It isn't much," he says. "Or at least if there's anything important here, I don't know what it is."

I head down to Sam's office to get a look at it myself, and it's quite a sight. Eli, Hilda, Leon, and Morris are hunched over computers, although the truth is that they could be standing up and still look as if they're hunched.

Sam sits at his own desk, peering at his workers like a lazy factory foreman. He's also drinking coffee and eating what look like small pastries. "They're called rugelach," Sam says. "Hilda made them; they're unbelievable."

Since I see myself as a hands-on attorney, I eat a half dozen of them, and they are truly fantastic. Once Sam and I have polished off all of them, I ask to see what they've got.

It's amazing what can be learned using a computer, especially when those using it have no qualms about entering sites they have no legal right to be in. What Sam's team has is impressive, whether it proves meaningful or not. Not quite as impressive as the rugelach, but that would be asking a lot.

What they have is a list of everyone whose phone was connected to Gerald Downey's phone in the last month of Downey's life, whichever phone made the call. There is also information about each of those people, including address, occupation, family status, financial data, arrest and criminal records, and everything else available online.

If it weren't so fascinating that they could put this together, it would be scary. Privacy is a quaint little concept that no longer has any relevance in the modern world. The other scary thing is that Hilda and Eli Mandlebaum, both born during the Hoover administration, know more about the modern world than I do.

There are three phones that Downey was in contact with that were the kind you buy in stores without a contract, so there are no names attached to them. Sam's gang was able to identify where the phones were purchased, but not who did the purchasing.

Sam gives me a folder with printouts of all the information, and it actually consumes twenty pages. I'll take it home and read through it, which is not something I particularly look forward to. With the trial looming, I still have to spend a lot of time familiarizing myself with all the evidence.

"This is great, guys," I say.

"There's more," Sam says, handing me another, thinner folder. "It's Eric Brantley's travel records. Where he went, when he went there, the purpose of the visit, where he stayed, what airline he took, all of it."

"You guys are amazing."

He nods. "Yes, we are."

There isn't that much I like about my job. I don't want anyone to think being a trial lawyer is terrible, because it isn't. There are worse things I could be doing. I don't work outside in ten-degree weather, I don't toil in the field picking crops in the heat of summer, and I'm not an usher at the opera.

Probably the thing I like most about lawyering is cross-examination. My absolute favorite is to catch an adversarial witness in a lie, and beat him over the head with it. When I have that kind of witness on the stand, I love to badger, humiliate, and verbally torture him. Other than that I'm really quite sweet.

But to be able to experience that intense pleasure, I have to do the thing I hate the most about my job, which is to study. I have to be completely familiar with every piece of evidence, no matter how seemingly insignificant it might be. Because the key to effective cross-examination, and for that matter to effective lawyering, is to have a total grasp of the facts, and to be able to instantly summon them.

That is why I spend every night in the pretrial and trial phase going over and over the relevant documents. Most of it is tedious and dry, but it's essential to have a complete command of it.

Sometimes I can read a document for the fifth time and suddenly see something significant that I missed the first four. But that is a rare happening, and tonight is unfortunately not one of those nights.

I take a break from my reading to put Ricky to bed. Once I get to his room, he holds up a pair of my socks, ones that I have given him just for this purpose. His holding it up is a silent challenge to engage him in my favorite sport growing up, sock basketball.

"I'm going to destroy you," I say.

Ricky just nods his annoyingly confident nod. "Bring it on."

The idea is to shoot the rolled-up socks onto the ledge above the door. We don't dribble, since socks are not dribble-able, but we pretend to. I'm five-eleven, and Ricky is probably four-something, so I have a fairly significant height advantage. I also outweigh him by at least a hundred pounds.

The energy and stamina advantages are his.

We don't keep track of wins and losses, but a good guess would be that I've lost probably fifty games in a row. I've been close in some, but he always seems to come through at the end. I am the Washington Generals of sock basketball.

Tonight we're tied with five seconds to go in the game, and he has the sock. He takes a shot and misses, and calls a foul.

"Foul?" I whine. "Are you crazy?"

"You hit me on the arm," he says, and casually hits the game-winning foul shot. "Sorry, Dad," he says, the same thing he says at the end of every game we play. "You almost had me."

"I'll get you next time, Rick" is always my response.

I tuck him in and kiss him on the forehead. "I love you, Dad," he says. He doesn't say it every night, but when he does, I am always stunned by how good words can feel.

"I love you, too, son," I say. Bedtime is the only time I call him son; all other times it's Rick or Ricky. I'm not sure why that is, and I really don't care very much. It feels right.

I head into the den, passing Laurie on the way. "You lose again?" she asks.

I nod. "I should have won. Ref made a bad call."

I go back into the den to continue reading, then realize that I left some documents on the dresser in Ricky's room. As I tiptoe in to retrieve them, I hear a strange noise.

The strange noise is Ricky crying in bed. My instinct is to run and get Laurie, but I fight it off. "What's the matter, Rick? What's wrong?" I ask.

"Nothing."

I'd love to leave it at that, but I can't. "Come on, something's bothering you. Maybe I can help make it better."

"No . . . you can't."

"Try me," I say.

"I miss my dad."

"I know you do, Rick. And you're right: I can't make that better. I wish I could, more than anything."

"I'm starting to forget things about him. I remember stuff, but then it goes away," he says.

"What's important is to remember that he loves you, and that you love him. And your mom and I love you, too."

"Okay," he says, but I don't think he agrees with my assessment of what's important. He thinks what's important is that his real father is dead, and he'll never see him again.

I may be learning what it's like to literally ache for someone. "You want Mom to come in?" I ask.

"I want to go to sleep."

I kiss him goodnight and go into the den. Laurie is in there, and I tell her about the conversation with Ricky. She's had a number of them, and reassures me that I did okay. I'm not sure I agree with her.

She pours me a glass of wine, which is on the table next to my recliner chair. I sip it as I go through the documents; with any luck, I'll fall asleep in the middle of my reading.

The materials are just as dry and boring as they were earlier in the evening, but I stay awake. Eventually I switch over to the information that Sam and his team have given me about Downey and his recent contacts.

The names of the people on the list are just names to me, and the information that Sam's team has gathered about each of them doesn't really bring them to life. Very little about them piques my interest; even those with criminal records are small-time, and their crimes don't really relate to this case.

All of that is true until I get to Gino Parelli. By the time I reach his name I am in skimming mode, and I almost go right past it. And it may not mean anything, but his occupation, listed as "Customs Official, Port Newark," jumps off the page at me.

I'm not an expert on smuggling things into the country, diamonds or anything else, but my guess is that very little of it comes into places like Des Moines or Omaha. It most likely comes into our ports, and one of those is Port Newark.

I have no idea whether Parelli has anything to do with this case; for all I know he and Downey could have been on the same bowling team. But I'm going to find out.

In the meantime, I move on to reading Brantley's travel records. He certainly didn't get away much, and it appears none of the trips he did take were vacations. He'd been to three conferences in the past two years: one in Cleveland, one in San Francisco, and one in Zurich.

The Zurich trip was a conference sponsored by an international organization of chemists, of which Brantley was a member. The fact that it took place almost a year ago makes it moderately interesting to me, but not as interesting as one other fact that Hilda has uncovered. Rather than fly directly home, Brantley flew to Johannesburg, where he spent three days. Johannesburg is known to be a key city in the diamond world.

I call Sam and ask him to check Brantley's and Downey's phone records for the thirty days after Brantley returned to the United States. There is no way to know why Brantley went to South Africa, or whether it has anything concrete to do with our case.

But it sure as hell is interesting.

Add "dockworker" to the list of jobs I don't want to have. I wouldn't like it any day, but especially not one like today, when the temperature is approaching ninety degrees. Just going from my car to the docks feels like I'm tightrope walking on the equator. And though just being out here is bad enough, the prospect of adding manual labor to the situation makes this one of those rare times I'm glad I went to law school.

I reach what seems to be a main building, but is really only a warehouse. I walk inside, and am surprised and delighted to discover that it is air-conditioned. I see a guy in a white shirt, holding a clipboard and writing on it. Clipboards seem to imply that the holder knows what he or she is doing, so I approach the guy. "I'm looking for Gino Parelli," I say.

"Ask me if I give a shit," he says, without looking up or stopping his writing.

"Do you give a shit?"

He writes a little more, then looks up. "Nope," he says.

"I'm glad we cleared that up. Do you know where Parelli is?"

He looks at the clipboard. "Dock fifteen."

I point to the dock just outside the building. "Which one is this?"

"That would be dock one," he says, meaning I've got a really long walk to dock fifteen.

"Any chance they count by twos?"

"Nope. But you could drive there."

That being the best idea I've heard in a while, I get in my car and drive down to dock fifteen. Had I attempted to walk it in this heat, I would never have been heard from again.

When I get there, I am disappointed to discover that not only is there not an air-conditioned building, but there is actually no building at all. I find another clipboard person, this time a woman, and she points out Parelli, who is apparently taking a break, sitting on a bench and smoking a cigarette.

"Gino Parelli?" I ask as I approach him.

"Yeah?" It's more of a question than a response, but it's asked warily, so I take it as a yes.

"My name is Andy Carpenter. I'm an attorney, and I'd like to talk to you about Gerald Downey," I say.

"What about him?" he asks. In situations like this I don't call ahead and arrange a meeting, because I want to see how people react without having time to prepare. In the case of Parelli, there is a clear look of either fear or worry on his face.

"Your relationship with him."

"I don't know any Gerald Downey."

He's lying. I know that because if he really didn't know Downey, his response would have been "Who's that?" or "Never heard of him." His first response would not have been to ask, "What about him?" It's like if someone calls and asks for you when you answer the phone, once you ask "Who's calling?" you can't later claim they got a wrong number.

"Boy, that's weird," I say. "You don't know him, but you helped him smuggle diamonds into the country?"

"That's bullshit," he says, but his tone is still more fear than anger. "Get out of here."

"Have you ever testified under oath, Gino?"

"I said get out of here. I'm not talking to you."

"Wrong again, Gino. You'll be talking to me in a courtroom." I look up at the sun. "An air-conditioned courtroom."

Once I'm in the cool comfort of my car, I call Sam Willis. "There's a guy named Gino Parelli, and—"

Sam interrupts. "He was on the Downey call list. What about him?"

"I want you to give him a cyber rectal exam."

You're about to find out that being a juror is a tough job" is how Dylan starts his opening remarks. I can sense Tommy sitting up slightly higher in his seat. This is it, it's showtime.

We have been through three days of jury selection and some pretrial bullshit. I'm sure it felt to Tommy like we'd never get to the actual trial, but we're here now, and he's happier about it than I am. That's probably because I know the state of our case.

"First of all, it goes against our grain," Dylan continues. "Haven't our parents, and our teachers, and our friends always told us that it's somehow wrong to judge other people? Isn't that somehow beneath us?

"Well, let me deal with that right here and now. You are not judging Thomas Infante; that's not your job. You are trying to determine whether or not he committed a particular act, and you are trying to do so beyond a reasonable doubt. Once you have determined that, it is for others to judge, and others to punish, should that be called for.

"But secondly, there is a lot of pressure on you; you are probably feeling it already. Because you do not live in a vacuum, you know full well that Mr. Infante's future is at stake, and riding on what you determine to be the true facts.

"And it is a lot of pressure, and everyone in this courtroom feels it. But you must put that aside, and let the facts lead you. Because they call this 'jury duty' for a reason: you have a duty to your fellow citizens, and to yourselves, to do your best to get this right.

"Many, many people have been in your situation, and have faced what you are facing. I sympathize with you, but on some level I envy you. You have a chance to contribute to your community, your state, and your country.

"I would submit that your task is actually easier than many others have faced. Sometimes juries are confronted with extraordinarily complicated cases that seem to defy a simple yes or no. But as you will see when the facts unfold before you, this case is fairly straightforward.

"You are being asked to determine whether or not Thomas Infante murdered Gerald Downey. The state of New Jersey, and myself personally, believe that he did so, well beyond a reasonable doubt. We will, through our witnesses, tell you exactly why we feel that way.

"I am confident that you will agree, and I am equally confident that you will do your duty. Thank you."

It was a very low-key opening statement by Dylan, probably the most evenhanded I have ever heard him give. I have no doubt that it's because he truly is confident in his case and the ability of the jury to understand it.

Judge Klingman gives me the opportunity to deliver my opening statement now, or defer it to the start of our case. As always, I opt to do it now, so that the jury can understand we are not about to roll over.

I stand up and steal a glance at the gallery and media assembled behind me. Time has eroded some of the "glamor" of the near-decapitation death, and there are a number of empty seats in the courtroom. It doesn't much matter to me either way; this case was not the type that was going to be unduly influenced by media or public pressure.

"Mr. Campbell and I will agree on almost nothing throughout the course of this trial. It is the nature of the process: he has his job and his point of view, and I have mine. We are adversaries, and this is an adversarial proceeding.

"But we do agree on a couple of things, so let's get those agreeable items out of the way, so we can move on. We agree that you have a duty to perform, and it is an admirable one that entails a lot of pressure, because much is at stake.

"We also agree on something that he didn't mention in his statement, that Thomas Infante has never been in this position before. I don't mean that he has never been tried for murder; I mean that he has never been tried for anything. Never tried, never convicted, never arrested. Never.

"But Mr. Campbell and I strongly disagree on the difficulty of the task ahead of you. This is not a simple case, and by the time it is over you will not be able to understand how he could describe it that way. Because while this murder took place in New Jersey, the process of understanding it will take you to the far corners of the world.

"You will be asked to understand and consider a massive international conspiracy, involving remarkable amounts of money and violence. And you will find that this is way bigger than Gerald Downey, and way bigger than Thomas Infante.

"Simple?" I smile my wryest smile. "I don't think so, and you won't either."

I sit down, first patting Tommy on the shoulder in a gesture of support. I would be feeling reasonably good about my statement, except for the fact that I have no confidence I can back it up. I wish the jury could cast their votes now, because this might be our high point.

In a perfect world, Judge Klingman would say, "Mr. Carpenter, that was such an extraordinary opening statement that I am declaring your client innocent. On behalf of the state of New Jersey I would like to thank you for being such a brilliant lawyer."

Instead, what he says is what I have been dreading. "Mr. Campbell, you may call your first witness."

"Captain Stanton, you were the first police officer on the scene?" Dylan asks.

Pete nods. "I was."

"What made you enter the house?"

"I had probable cause that a robbery had been committed. Mr. Downey was a suspect."

Dylan has called Pete to establish the foundation; he needs him to set the scene. It's something he had to do, but likely not something he was relishing.

"Please describe what you saw when you entered the house."

"Mr. Downey was sitting in a chair. His throat had been cut to the point that his head was barely on his torso. There was a dog sitting near Mr. Downey."

"Did you search the house?"

"I didn't personally, but some of my officers did."

"Did it appear as if a robbery had taken place?"

"It did not."

Dylan asks him a few more questions about procedure, and then turns him over to me.

"Captain Stanton, who was with you when you entered Mr. Downey's house?"

"You were, and Willie Miller; you had called me to report the robbery."

"And what did we say had been stolen?"

"You believed that Mr. Downey had stolen a dog from your rescue foundation. The GPS on the dog's collar had led you to that house."

"Did we hear barking when we rang the doorbell?"

He nods. "Yes, Willie Miller said he was positive that the barking was that of the stolen dog. That's what gave me the probable cause to enter."

"When you were in the house, did you get a good look at the dog?" I ask.

"I did."

I walk back to the defense table, and Hike hands me an envelope. I take some photographs out of it and bring them to Judge Klingman. I ask him to admit them as defense exhibits, and Dylan agrees, albeit reluctantly. He knows what is coming, but doesn't want to object in advance, since he would lose, and it would look to the jury as if he has something to hide.

"Captain Stanton, is that the dog that was in Mr. Downey's house?"

"It certainly looks like her."

Dylan stands up. "Objection, Your Honor. Captain Stanton just spent a few minutes with that dog. There is no way he can make a positive identification."

The judge turns to me. "Mr. Carpenter?"

"Your Honor, I would like to continue; there will be testimony later confirming the identification beyond any doubt."

"Very well. Objection overruled."

I turn back to Pete. "In the first three pictures, can you tell who that is holding the dog's leash?"

Dylan objects again, but is again overruled. The judge tells Pete that he may answer.

"Yes, that is Eric Brantley," he says.

I feign surprise. "The Eric Brantley who was wanted for murder, and who was himself murdered?"

Dylan jumps up and objects, but hasn't a legal leg to stand on.

I smile. "I'm sorry, Your Honor, but with all the Eric Brantleys running around, I wanted to make sure we were talking about the same one."

Klingman seems to have trouble containing a smile, but he manages. "There are a lot of Eric Brantleys running around?" he asks.

I nod. "Throw a dart out your window and you're sure to hit one."

Klingman tells Pete he can answer the question, and he confirms that it is the now-deceased Eric Brantley.

"Do you know why Gerald Downey stole Eric Brantley's dog?"

"No, I don't," Pete says.

"Do you know what their relationship with each other was?"

"No."

"Do you know who killed Eric Brantley?"

"No."

"Do you know where Thomas Infante was when Eric Brantley was killed?"

"Yes. He was in jail."

"Thank you, Captain."

I love watching jurors' faces when Janet Carlson is on the witness stand. She is beautiful, to the point where she is in Laurie's class, and believe me, that is an honors class. In any event, she's the best-looking witness in any trial she's a part of.

But that is not what is so striking about the jurors' reaction to her. Janet is the county coroner, so she is often called upon to give graphic, sometimes pretty disgusting, descriptions of bodies she has examined. It just seems weird coming out of her mouth, even to me, and I've seen her do it many, many times.

It's in Dylan's best interest to make this murder appear as heinous as possible, and considering the circumstances, that's not too difficult. He's effectively using Janet to make his point.

"So you would describe this as a near decapitation?" Dylan asks, even though she has previously described it that way twice during this testimony.

"Yes, I would."

"How many cut marks were made?"

"You mean how many times was the knife used?" she asks.

"Yes."

"At least four or five; the blade was apparently not very sharp."

"So would you say it was almost like a sawing, and not a slicing?" Dylan asks.

She nods. "That's a fair statement."

"Did you find any other wounds or bruises?"

"A few facial lacerations," she says. "Some scrape marks where his hands were cuffed behind him."

"Was the victim conscious while all this was happening?"

"I see no reason to believe otherwise," she says. "I think the answer to that is almost definitely yes."

Dylan doesn't say anything for a few moments, no doubt letting the horror of what Janet is describing sink into the jurors' minds. Then he says, "No further questions."

I don't have much to get out of Janet; her testimony was merely a recitation of the facts. There's nothing new here; the jury already knew that Downey was murdered, and they knew the way he was murdered.

Her negative impact, from our point of view, was emotional. The jury had to be horrified by the graphic description they heard, and their natural instinct will be to punish someone for it. Unfortunately, the only person they have available to punish is Tommy Infante.

"That's a horrible way to die" is how I start my cross-examination. I'm not telling anyone in the courtroom anything they don't already know; I am merely establishing that the defense shares their feelings. I am telling them that in fact Tommy Infante shares their feelings, because he had as little to do with this crime as they did.

"Certainly was," Janet agrees.

"Would the killer have to have been particularly strong to do this?" I ask. Since Tommy is a large man, I want to establish that significant strength was not necessary.

"No, I wouldn't say so, since the victim was bound and therefore unable to resist."

"And if the killer was able to threaten with a gun or knife, handcuffing the victim to the chair wouldn't have taken great strength either, would it?"

"I wouldn't think so."

"Based on the angle, would the killer have to have been tall?" Tommy is six foot four.

"No, because Mr. Downey was sitting in a chair. Any normal-sized person would have been angling the knife downward."

"And you said the killer was in front of his victim when he attacked him?"

"Yes."

"Would there have been a lot of blood?" I ask.

She nods. "Absolutely. The jugular was sliced."

"Any way the killer could have avoided getting blood on his clothing?"

"That would not be possible, no."

I let Janet off the stand. I've accomplished what I needed to, and will take advantage of it later in the trial.

recognize the face as soon as I see it on the screen. It's Professor Charles Horowitz, Eric Brantley's boss at Markham College. I don't have to wait to hear what the newscaster is saying, because there's a banner across the screen that says it all:

BRANTLEY PROFESSOR MISSING

For some reason the first thing that flashes across my mind is that a noted professor is missing, but in their banner they've reduced the poor guy to nothing more than a player in the Brantley case.

I've just woken up, and since Laurie is still sleeping, I have the sound on mute. Since I need to hear what is being said, I turn the sound up to a level I can hear, but that hopefully will not wake her. It doesn't work. In an instant she's up and watching with me.

The announcer is saying that Horowitz hasn't shown up for four days, which is completely uncharacteristic for him. No one has seen him since he left work a few nights ago, and he has not used his phone. His car is in his driveway, but he's not in the house.

The police have classified Horowitz as a missing person,

which isn't exactly an earthshaking announcement, since he is a person, and he is missing. If they have any idea how or if it actually ties in to the Brantley case, they clearly haven't shared it with this announcer.

When he's finished, I say to Laurie, "That's the guy I met with."

She nods. "I know. Any reason to think he's a threat to anyone?"

"No, but I really don't have a clue. He could also be on the run."

"Unlikely," she says, "if he drove home and left his car there. He could have rented one, but he had to have a way to get to the rental place. That leaves a trail, as would the rental itself."

I look online for more information, which is something I find myself doing more and more frequently these days. Television, despite the proliferation of twenty-four-hour news channels, just doesn't provide the in-depth coverage that can be found online.

Unfortunately, my online search doesn't turn up many more details about Horowitz's disappearance. Apparently the police are not sharing information, and it's too early in the process for reporters to have dug up much.

There is one unconfirmed report that is interesting. It talks of an investigation going on at Markham College over some missing equipment from the labs. The implication, which as far as I can tell is unsubstantiated, is that perhaps Horowitz had something to do with it. I guess the theory is that he went on the run rather than deal with the repercussions of his theft, but that doesn't really seem plausible to me.

Horowitz had spent years educating himself and attaining a respected position in the academic world. The idea that he would steal some equipment and blow it all seems far-fetched, and is not consistent with how he came across to me. There is no doubt in my mind that Horowitz's disappearance is tied to Brantley.

But obviously I could be wrong.

The irritating, and scary, thing about this situation is that even if I'm right it won't matter. The only place I've established a connection between Brantley and the Downey murder is in my own mind. I am nowhere close to getting Judge Klingman to allow the jury to hear about it.

Before I even get out of bed, I call Sam. Once again he answers on the first ring, but instead of saying "hello," he says, "Horowitz?"

"You got it," I say. I don't have to tell Sam what I want; he knows I want him to dig into Horowitz's life, especially the last few months. I want to know everyone he's talked to, as well as where he has been.

I get up to take Tara and Sebastian on their morning walk; it's Saturday, so I can take a long one without worrying about making it to court. Before I can get out the door, the phone rings. To my surprise, Tommy Infante is on the line.

It's the first time he has ever called me from the jail, so the first thing I say is, "Tommy, all calls from the jail are monitored. Do not say anything you don't want everyone to hear."

"I'm on a cell," he says.

"You have a cell phone?"

"You obviously haven't spent much time in jail" is his way of telling me what I actually already knew, that the black market in jail provides cell phones to anyone who wants it.

"Be careful anyway," I say. "Is this important? You want me to come down there?"

He doesn't answer that, but instead asks a question of his own. "What does Horowitz mean?"

"I don't know yet," I say. "I'm looking into it now."

"He's dead."

He says it with a certainty that surprises me. "What makes you say that?"

"Because everybody's dead. Downey, Brantley, Caruso, Healy . . . they're all dead and I might as well be dead sitting in here."

The stress in his voice is evident, and much more intense than I've heard before. "You okay?" I ask.

"Yeah. I'm okay," he says. "I'm an okay dead man, sitting in a cell. Do we have any chance to win this thing?"

"If we didn't I would have suggested you plead it out. But it's an uphill climb."

"I'm going crazy in here," he says. Then, "I gotta go. Somebody's coming."

He hangs up. I've never heard him this upset; until now he's handled his situation remarkably well. I certainly don't blame him; I'm upset myself, but more than that, I'm scared.

I'm scared that I won't be able to help him, and I'm scared of living with that failure afterward.

nd you were working on the night in question?" Dylan asks. He's questioning Dan Hendricks, the bartender Marcus and I visited with at the Study Hall bar. He's already established that the night they are talking about is the one where Tommy Infante and Gerald Downey were in the bar together.

Hendricks nods. "Yeah. It was a Monday." Apparently he assumes that everyone in the courtroom is familiar with his work schedule.

"Did the defendant and Mr. Downey enter the bar together?"

"No. Gerry was there first; he came in about ten minutes later."

"By 'he,' you mean the defendant?" Dylan asks.

"Right. The defendant."

"And they were talking to each other?"

"Yeah," Hendricks says. "He . . . the defendant . . . went right over to Gerry."

"Could you hear what they were saying?"

"Are you kidding? Everybody could hear them. He was screaming at Gerry."

"What was he saying?" Dylan asks.

"I don't remember some of the exact words, but he said that he and Gerry robbed some jewelry store, and that Gerry never gave him his share."

"And he was upset about that?"

Hendricks laughs a short laugh. "Oh, yeah. He was real upset."

"How do you know that?"

"He was screaming, you know? And he kept telling Gerry that if he didn't get his money, he would slit his throat."

"Do you remember his exact words?"

Hendricks nods. "I sure do. He kept screaming, 'I'm going to slit your goddamn throat.' He must have said it five times."

Dylan wants these words to be the last ones the jury hears on direct examination, so he ends his questioning on that note, and turns the witness over to me.

"Were you there when the police arrived?" is my first question.

"What do you mean?"

"I'm talking about that night, after the argument broke out. If you were still there, what happened when the police came?"

"They didn't come."

"Did you leave before they got there?" I ask.

"I closed the place. There were no police."

"So the defendant was there, screaming at the top of his lungs and threatening murder, and nobody called the police?"

"No."

"Not even Mr. Downey?"

"Nah. Gerry didn't seem too worried about it, so I guess nobody else was. A couple of the guys just threw the guy . . . the defendant . . . out."

"Did Gerry say why he never gave the defendant his share of the stolen property?"

"He said the guy was nuts, that they never robbed no store. He said he only met the defendant a few times, and really didn't know him that well."

"Did that surprise you?"

"Yeah, I guess. But it's none of my business, you know?"

"Did Mr. Downey seem worried to you?"

"Nah. He just kept saying that the guy was nuts."

"How many people were in the bar when this argument took place?" I ask.

"I'm not sure. Maybe twenty."

"And everyone there heard these threats?"

"Unless they were deaf."

"The defendant didn't try and prevent anyone from hearing them?"

"No way."

I'm trying to convey to the jury that it's illogical to think that someone who intended to slit someone's throat would announce it in advance for the world to hear. It's a weak argument, but in the context of this witness, it's all we've got.

"No further questions."

I never have trouble sleeping. I'm not sure why that is, but no matter what is going on in my personal or work life, no matter how great or miserable things are, it doesn't affect my ability to zonk out.

Tonight is going to test that premise. It's not that I might lie awake because I'm upset that the case is going so badly, although I am. It's not the pressure of watching Tommy Infante, in my view an innocent man, go down the judicial drain, although that pressure is severe.

Tonight my problem is that there is something in the back of my mind, and I can't seem to move it to the front. It's been bugging me all day, just staying out of reach. I feel like I know something important, but for the life of me I can't figure out what the hell it is.

Sometimes these things come to me, and sometimes they don't. I've learned that I can't push it; when I don't try to come up with it, I have more success than when I do. And occasionally when I do figure it out, and analyze it, it can turn out to be insignificant. I just won't know until I know.

For some reason the shower is a place where stuff can sometimes pop into my head, so tonight I take one before heading for bed. Thirty minutes later I'm like a prune, but my mind is just as blank as when I was dry.

So I get into bed, and the torment and pressure cause me to toss and turn for almost a minute before I'm sound asleep. I wake up at 3:17; I check the clock because for some reason I want to note the time I've come up with the thing that was bothering me. And it's a beauty.

Tommy Infante is guilty.

The realization of it is so intense and stunning that I get up and pace around the room. I almost step on Sebastian in the dark, and though he lets out a low growl, he doesn't consider the intrusion worthy of getting up over.

"Are you okay?" Laurie asks. I'm not sure if it was my pacing or Sebastian's growl, but it was obviously enough to wake her up, and she sits up slightly.

"It's something I just realized about the case," I say. "But go back to sleep; we can talk about it in the morning."

"Okay," she says, and lies back down.

"You're not going to believe it," I say.

She sighs, knowing where this is heading. "Am I not going to believe it now, or in the morning?"

"You're not going to believe it now . . . it's a disaster."

She turns on the lamp and sits all the way up. "What is it?"

"Tommy Infante is guilty. He killed Downey."

"What? How do you know that?"

"Tommy called me the other day; he had heard about Horowitz being missing, and he was very upset. He said that Horowitz was dead."

"How does he know that?" she asks.

I nod. "That's what I asked him. He never really answered except to say that they were all dead . . . Downey, Brantley,

Caruso, and Healy. He said that he might as well be dead as well."

"He's under a lot of stress, Andy. People say things."

"That's what I attributed it to," I say. "But it's more than that, and I missed it until tonight."

"What is it?"

"One of the people he mentioned as being dead was Healy."

"So?" she asks.

"So how does he know Healy? They've never released his name publicly; I only know it because the customs guy told me. And you're the only person I've told it to. How could he possibly have known that Healy was the one murdered with Brantley?"

"And you're sure he mentioned Healy?" she asks.

"I'm positive. And I'm just as positive that I never mentioned it to him."

"So how could he have found out?"

"He's got a cell phone; he called me on it. Those calls aren't monitored, so someone on the outside must have told him. And maybe that same person told him about Horowitz, and it scared him. He knows who he's dealing with, and he's scared he'll be next."

"Okay, let's assume he found out about Healy that way. That means he's somehow involved with the people behind all this. But it doesn't necessarily mean he killed Downey."

"Really? Which way are you betting?"

She thinks for a moment. Then, "That he killed him."

We talk for a few more minutes before Laurie asks me the obvious question. "What are you going to do?"

"I'm going to ask him about it. It's too late for me to get him brought to court early, so I'll have to meet with him during the lunch break."

"You think he'll be straight with you?"

"I don't know."

"What if he admits that he did it? What will you do then?"

"I don't know that either." Pretty much the only thing I do know is that it's going to be a really long day.

There is no way out of this trial for me. That is an unfortunate fact no matter what Tommy says when I confront him. I can file a motion to remove myself, but the judge would have to approve it, and there is no chance he would do so.

I never wanted a client in the first place, but I took on Tommy mainly because I thought he was innocent. If he's not, which is how it looks to me at the moment, then it's my version of a judicial nightmare.

My client's guilt would never be seen by the judge as a proper reason to bow out; guilty people are as entitled to a defense as innocent people. Not only that, but I could never reveal Tommy's guilt to the judge; it's privileged information that as his attorney I am obviously bound to keep confidential.

In any event, I'm on thin legal ice here. I should not be trying to discover whether Tommy is in fact definitely guilty. The problem is that if I know that, then I am ethically bound not to elicit testimony from him that is opposite to that. Should he testify in his own defense, I can't have him vow his innocence, if I know otherwise.

Having said that, I simply have to know the truth, and one way or the other, I'm going to find out what that truth is.

Tommy is brought into court about five minutes before the judge is due, and I greet him normally. I don't want to give him any hint that anything could be wrong, because I don't want him to have time to prepare a reaction or a story. Almost as important as what he will say to me is how he will look and act when he's saying it.

Tommy seems more stressed than usual. It's become a ritual for him to ask at the start of the court session, "Anything good going to happen today?" but this time he doesn't.

Dylan calls Sergeant Kevin Agnese, who conducted the search at Tommy's house. Agnese will be a relatively straightforward witness; he did nothing extraordinary or controversial. I know him very well; he and Pete have got to be the two biggest Mets fans in America.

"You entered the defendant's premises with a legal search warrant?" Dylan asks.

"Yes, sir."

"Did you find anything significant to this crime in your execution of the warrant?"

"We did. We found a knife with bloodstains on it."

"Did tests show it to be Gerald Downey's blood?"

I could object to this, since Agnese did not conduct the tests, but Dylan can introduce it easily enough through another witness. I don't want it to appear to the jury that I'm trying to hide any facts, especially since those facts will come in anyway. So I let the question slide.

"They did," Agnese says.

"Where did you find the knife?"

"Buried in the dirt in Mr. Infante's backyard."

Dylan asks a few more questions, but Agnese has really nothing else to offer him, so Dylan turns him over to me.

"Sergeant Agnese, was this the first time you've ever executed a search warrant?" I ask.

"No, sir. I've done many of them, probably a hundred."

"So you're good at it? You're very thorough?"

"Yes, I think so."

"Did you find anything else related to this case besides the knife?" I ask.

"No."

"Nothing in the house?"

"No."

"And you dug up the entire property?"

"No, sir. Just the area where the knife was."

I feign surprise. "Really? Why did you dig there?"

"We could see the earth had been tampered with," he says. "The knife was only an inch or two beneath the surface."

"So it was obvious? Little effort was made to conceal it?"

"I can't say what effort was made."

"Let's put it this way. If the person who buried it was trying to conceal it, they did a poor job?"

He doesn't want to, but he finally agrees with my point.

"Was the dirt hard there?" I ask.

"Not very."

"So without much effort, it could have been buried deeper?"

"I suppose so," Agnese admits.

"If you know, were there any fingerprints on the knife?"

"There were not."

"How far is Mr. Infante's house from Mr. Downey's?" I ask.

Agnese thinks for a moment. "I didn't measure it, but I would guess about six miles."

I nod. "So just to recap, according to your testimony, Mr. Infante would have murdered Mr. Downey, and rather than throw away the knife along the six-mile route to his home, he brought it to his own backyard? Even though it was not a knife that could be tied to him in any way, other than where it was found?"

"I'm just saying what I found," Agnese says.

"Right. Now you haven't mentioned the clothes. We've had testimony that there would have had to be blood on the clothes. Did you find them?"

"No, we did not."

"So if Mr. Infante committed the crime, he threw the clothes away elsewhere, but brought the knife home?"

"I can't say."

"You think the knife had special sentimental value?"

"I don't know," Agnese says, clearly getting frustrated.

I move toward him, talking louder and sounding a little angry. "But does any of that make sense to you?"

"That's not for me to judge," he says.

I nod. "Correct. It's for this jury to judge. No further questions."

The good news is that I think I did fairly well for my client. The bad news is that I think I did fairly well for my client.

When the judge adjourns for lunch, I turn to Tommy and say, "We have to talk."

"Something wrong?" he asks.

"We'll know soon enough."

W ho is Healy?" I ask as soon as he sits down in the anteroom.

"What do you mean?" is his lame response. Based on the look of fear on his face, he knows exactly what I mean.

"It's not really that confusing a question," I say. "I want to know who Healy is."

"I don't know."

"Then how did you know he was dead?"

"Hey, what's going on?" he asks. "What is this all about?"

"This is about me trying to find out how you knew about Healy, and how you know he is dead."

"I don't remember; maybe you told me. Or maybe I heard it on the radio. What's the difference?"

"I did not tell you," I say. "And it hasn't been on the radio, or the television, or anywhere else. Now are you going to tell me, or not?"

"I don't know, Andy. I heard it somewhere."

I stand up. "Maybe your next lawyer will believe your bullshit." It's a bluff; there's no way for me to get out of this case.

I start for the door, hoping Tommy will stop me before I get there. "Wait a minute, Andy. Please come back here."

I turn and come back, once again sitting in the chair. I don't say anything; I don't have to. The ball is in his court, and he knows it.

"I knew Healy; I did some work for him last year."

"What kind of work?" I ask.

"At the port in Newark. We unloaded some boxes out of crates, and put 'em onto a truck. He paid me five thousand dollars."

"For unloading some boxes?"

He nods. "It was at two o'clock in the morning."

"How did he come to hire you?"

"Through Downey; Downey was his boy. According to Downey, he did a lot of work for Healy."

"Does the name Gino Parelli mean anything to you?" I ask.

He thinks for a moment. "I think that was Downey's friend at the pier. He was in on it somehow."

"Keep going." I don't want to ask any questions; it might reveal how little I know. I want everything to come from him.

"Healy came to me about a week before Downey died. He said he knew my little girl was sick, and that I needed money, and he had a way to get me a lot of it. He told me to threaten Downey in the bar; he gave me a whole script to follow. He told me to threaten to slit his throat."

Tommy had once before mentioned a sick child, but I haven't seen any evidence that she exists, and at this point I have my doubts that she does. "Did he tell you why he wanted you to threaten him?"

"Just that Downey was starting to cause problems, and he wanted him to know that it wouldn't be tolerated."

"What about the jewelry store robbery?"

Tommy shakes his head. "There wasn't any; that was just something Healy told me to say. He said Downey would know what it was really about, and that he'd get the message."

"And you believed all this?"

"It didn't matter if I believed it. My kid is sick, and Healy paid me another five grand. Up front. So I did it, and then I heard that Downey got murdered, and the way it happened. . . . I did not do this, Andy."

"Did you talk to Healy after that?"

He nods. "I did. He told me that things didn't go down the way they were planned, and that I might be arrested. He said I wouldn't be in jail that long, that they would plant some evidence that would get me out. And he said they would get me a lawyer. That's why I asked if somebody sent you, that first day at the jail. Healy said I should trust him."

"And did you?"

"Of course not. But he sent my ex-wife another ten grand, and he told me that the best thing for the health of her and my kid was for me to sit tight. He was threatening them, and I couldn't protect them. This was a guy who had just slit somebody's throat, Andy."

"So you didn't tell anyone?"

He shakes his head. "No. What was I going to say? I had no idea where Healy was; would anybody believe my story?"

"Keep going."

"So then I heard about Brantley getting killed, and I knew that you thought my case was tied in to Brantley. So I called Healy, and somebody else answered."

"Who was it?"

"I don't know; it wasn't a voice I recognized. So I asked for Healy, and he told me that Healy was dead, and that if I said anything, the same thing would happen to me and my family. Then he told me not to call again, and he hung up. I was freaking out, but I didn't know what to do. I still don't."

I have no idea if Tommy is telling the truth or not, but one thing is for certain: he's not making this story up as he goes along. It's either true, or well prepared for the eventuality that I would confront him like this.

"What's your ex-wife's name, and where do they live?" I ask.

"You need to leave them out of this."

"Then you need to find a new lawyer." My theory is that empty threats are most effective when repeated.

He thinks for a moment, so I add, "You lied to me, Tommy. It's the one thing I can't tolerate."

He nods in what seems to be resignation. "Her name is Luann Willoughby; they live on Ridgetop Road in Morristown."

I ask him for the number he called Healy on, and he gives me that as well. "Okay," I say, and get up to leave.

"What are you going to do?" he asks.

"Just what I've been doing."

barely have time to call Laurie before the afternoon session begins. I tell her about my conversation with Tommy in detail, and ask her to have Sam check out some of the facts. Just before I hang up, she asks, "Do you believe him?"

"I'm embarrassed to say that I think I do. And if he is telling the truth, then he was stupid, but understandably so. And he doesn't deserve to be in jail."

The afternoon court session is going to be a relatively uneventful one. Dylan will be focusing on the forensics, which are incriminating, but will add very little to what the jury already knows.

First up is Sergeant Jessie McNab who handled the on-site forensics, both at Downey's house and Tommy's. Dylan takes way longer than necessary to bring out the only important details of the testimony, the fact that Tommy's fingerprints were in Downey's house, and Downey's blood was on the knife buried in Tommy's backyard.

My first question on cross is, "Sergeant, how many different sets of fingerprints did you find in Mr. Downey's house?"

"Eleven."

"If you know, how many of those eleven people were arrested for the murder?"

"One."

"Were my prints in the house?" I ask.

"Yes, they were on the front door and the staircase."

"Are you aware of any warrants out for my arrest?"

"No, but I can check when I get back to the station."

That gets a laugh out of everyone in the courtroom, including me, though I'm probably the only one fake laughing. "When did I leave my prints there?" I ask.

"That's not knowable from the prints themselves."

"Would that be true of Mr. Infante's prints as well?"

"Yes."

"You don't know when he left them there?" I ask.

"I do not."

"Sergeant McNab, are you aware of testimony that the two men knew each other?"

"I am."

"Did you find other evidence of Mr. Infante's presence in the house? Any DNA, for instance?"

"No."

"So, let me sum up what you've said about Mr. Infante's presence in the house, and tell me if I've mischaracterized it. Based on fingerprint evidence, and fingerprint evidence only, you can tell that at some point in history, Mr. Infante was in Mr. Downey's house."

"I'm not sure I'd say 'at some point in history.'"

"Sorry," I say. "How would you put it?"

"I guess I'd say he was in the house, but I can't say when."

I nod. "Perfect. Let's go with your version. Now, let's move on to Mr. Infante's house. Did you find anything relating to

Mr. Downey on that property or in the house, other than the knife?"

"Mr. Downey's fingerprints were there as well."

"Ah, so they must have visited each other?"

"I can't say."

"What kind of knife was it?" I ask.

"It was a kitchen knife, made by Spencer."

"Is that a rare type?"

"I don't believe so."

"If I told you it was sold at twenty-one different stores in Bergen County alone, would you agree with that?"

"I don't know."

I introduce a document into evidence showing that in fact it is sold at all those stores, and then move on. "Were Mr. Downey's prints on the knife?" There has already been testimony that they were not.

"No."

"But there was blood?"

"Yes."

"So you think Mr. Infante wiped off his fingerprints, but left the blood? Fingerprints on an ordinary kitchen knife found on his own property would be more incriminating than the victim's blood?"

"I don't know what he did, or why."

"Was there blood in the defendant's car?"

"No."

I feign surprise. "Not even from the knife?"

"No."

"No bloody clothes?"

"No."

"So he made sure the car was clean, and that there were no

fingerprints on the knife, but he then buried a bloody knife a half-inch deep on his own property? Is that your testimony?"

"I'm just telling you the facts."

"Thank you, Sergeant McNab. That's what we're looking for."

t all checks out, Andy," Sam says. "Her name is Luann Willoughby, and she lives in Morristown where Tommy said she lives. She and Tommy were divorced six years ago, and they have a ten-year-old daughter named Jenny."

Sam has come over to give Laurie and me the results of his efforts to check out what Tommy told me when I confronted him. "Is the daughter sick?" I ask.

He nods. "No question about it. She's been in the hospital on and off for almost a year."

"What's wrong with her?"

Sam shrugs, in what seems like his version of embarrassment. "I got the hospital records, but I didn't look at them. Didn't seem right."

"That's okay, Sam," Laurie says. "You did the right thing."

I nod. "Absolutely. And what about the money?"

"She made two large cash deposits, one was for five thousand, the other for ten thousand. No way to be sure where she got the money, but they match what Tommy told you."

I'm certainly glad that all of this checked out, but of course that doesn't prove anything. Tommy could have a sick child, and received money from Healy, just like he said, but that doesn't mean he didn't also murder Downey. In fact, ten thousand dollars seems like it would more likely be a payment for a hit than for simply walking into a bar and threatening someone.

Having said all that, my inclination is to believe Tommy. The story had the ring of truth, and this confirming information adds to its credibility, at least in my mind. It could be that I just want to believe him, since I'm stuck defending him, but it doesn't really matter either way. It is what it is.

Sam also brings another piece of interesting news. Shortly after Brantley returned from South Africa, he made three phone calls to Downey, and received two from him. Whatever connection he made over there probably had Downey's name as someone who could get him into the diamond world. It did not end well for either of them.

Sam leaves, and Ricky, Tara, Sebastian, and I go for our evening walk. Before Ricky and Sebastian were part of our family, Laurie would sometimes accompany Tara and me. She usually doesn't now; I've never asked her why, but I think she wants to give us some father-son bonding time.

Ricky is still grappling with the soccer versus baseball quandary, and I have tried to stay out of it and not be a pushy father. I've bought Ricky a new glove and bat, but that was not done to pressure him. Nor was the promise of a higher allowance if he plays baseball.

"Will Rubenstein thinks soccer is for wimps," he says.

"Will is a smart kid," I say. "Very, very bright."

"But I like both games; I don't know what to do."

"You know, you could try one, see how it goes, and then if you want, try the other."

"You think so?" he asks.

"Sure. For example, you could focus on baseball, and then in ten or fifteen years if you don't like it, we can talk about it."

"Mom thinks soccer is just as good."

"Mom's very smart, but she isn't really into sports like we guys are."

Ricky thinks for a moment, then says, "Okay, I think I'll play baseball first."

I'm not proud of what I've said, and I have a bad feeling about how I've handled this. Fortunately, I'll get over that feeling. "Sounds like a good idea, Rick."

"Should we talk to Mom about this when we get back?" he asks.

"I don't think so. She's pretty busy doing mother stuff."

When we get back, Laurie doesn't seem to be doing any mother stuff. Instead, she's waiting for us on the porch. And she wants to talk about something other than the baseball versus soccer controversy.

"Alan Divac is the guy you went to see about diamonds, right?" she asks.

"Right. Why?"

"He was arrested for diamond smuggling, money laundering, arms sales, and murder."

This is a stunner; I thought Divac represented the legitimate end of the diamond importing business. "Murder of who?" I ask.

"Michael Caruso, Brantley's partner. Now they're saying that they were wrong, that Brantley didn't do it. Divac either did it, or contracted it out."

"But they're not charging him with the murder of Brantley?"

"Apparently not," she says. "At least the media isn't reporting it."

I go inside and watch a news conference that CNN is broadcasting. The head agent for Immigration and Customs Enforcement is answering questions. In the background are Agents Hernandez and Gardiner. They had registered apparent surprise when I mentioned I had talked to Alan Divac; apparently they were preparing to drop the bomb on him at around that time.

The agent says, "There remains additional charges that may be filed at a future time, including, but not limited to, possible additional counts of homicide."

A short while later one of the reporters asks him if Divac will be the only one charged in the case, and his answer is, "The investigation is ongoing, and there may be charges filed against certain foreign nationals who are not named in this indictment."

"What about others within Divac's company?" is the next question.

He shakes his head. "At this point we do not anticipate others being implicated in the conspiracy. Mr. Divac was running this operation separate and apart from his company and its employees."

The press conference ends, and so does the coverage of the story. Laurie and I decide to wait until she puts Ricky to bed before we discuss what the development might mean for our case.

I pour us each a glass of wine while Laurie is in Ricky's room, tucking him in, and I hand one to her when she joins me in the den. "He loves going on those walks with you," she says.

"Is that what he said?"

"Yes."

"Did he say anything else?" I ask, fearful that he threw me under the baseball bus.

"Like what?"

"Nothing. Nothing at all."

Her antennae are obviously activated. "Is there something you're not telling me?"

"Are you kidding? No way. Just making conversation."

I can tell she doesn't believe me, but we move on to the news about Divac's arrest. "It can't help us," I say, ever upbeat. "It can only hurt."

"Why?"

"Well, for one thing, there's an air of finality to it, at least in our time frame. The investigations are for all intents and purposes over, and Divac will lawyer up. By the time he goes to trial, if he ever does, our boat will have sailed long ago."

"Maybe you can talk to those customs agents," she says. "I'm sure they know more than they'll say in a press conference."

"The problem is I don't have leverage with them anymore. They've got their man, so there's nothing they need from me. And we still haven't tied any of this to Downey's murder."

"So let's look at the big picture," Laurie says. "What is our theory on who committed these murders?"

"Well, Brantley had a relationship with Downey; we know that because Downey stole Zoe for him. So in my mind whoever killed one, killed the other. And I believe Brantley was trying to smuggle diamonds in, which would have made him a competitor of Divac's. So my best guess, and it's only a guess, is that Divac ordered the murders."

"Where does Healy come in?" she asks.

"That's even harder to figure. Based on what Tommy said about Healy getting him to threaten Downey, I assumed Healy must have killed Downey. So he would have likely targeted Brantley as well, but he was killed with Brantley."

"Maybe Healy turned on Divac," she says.

I nod. "Could be. And Divac brought that guy Alek in to clean up the whole mess and get rid of everybody."

"Including Brantley's boss? The professor?"

"Yes, if he was Brantley's partner in all this."

"Makes sense," she says. "But one other thing bothers me. Why would they have to frame Tommy for Downey's murder?"

I frown, which is what I do when I get frustrated. "This is just me guessing again, but maybe Divac wanted it to look like Downey's murder had nothing to do with the diamonds. That way the Feds wouldn't tie it in. And they set it up to look like Brantley killed his partner for the same reason."

"But why not have a fall guy for the Brantley and Healy murders?"

"Maybe because different people were doing the murders. Downey and Caruso were ordered by Divac. And whoever killed Brantley and Healy wanted Divac to take the fall for that, too. So they did frame someone; they framed Divac, but Divac is probably guilty."

"That also makes sense," she says.

"Yeah. But if we can't prove it, it doesn't help Tommy."

D ylan's final witness is basically here to make everyone sick. Her name is Dr. Collette Reny, and it definitely isn't her appearance that is the problem. She's no more than thirty-five, and strikingly pretty. She also talks in a soothing voice that projects intelligence and understanding. Nobody in the courtroom will have any problem believing she is a competent shrink.

She's been called to discuss the psychological ramifications of the way Gerald Downey died. The vicious slicing of the throat, as she points out, was not necessary to accomplish the goal of killing the victim. Nor is Dr. Reny's testimony necessary for Dylan to make his case. But having her there gives him a chance to again display the horrible crime scene photos in all their glory, allowing the jury to once more hate Tommy Infante for even being accused of doing such a thing.

I don't spend much time staring at the photos, since I experienced the scene live and in person. It is an image I am already having little success erasing from my mind; I don't need photographic reminders.

"It is clearly a demonstration of rage," Dr. Reny points out. "The killer wanted his victim to suffer, and the fact that the action was taken from the front means he wanted the victim to anticipate that suffering."

Dylan basically elicits this same testimony seven or eight times, to give the jury time to fully take it in. By the time he turns the witness over to me, half the jury probably wants to take Tommy out back and lynch him.

"Dr. Reny, when did you conduct your examination of Mr. Infante?"

"I did not have access to him," she says.

"Did you seek such access?"

"I did not."

"So you've never so much as talked to him?"

"I have not."

"Dr. Reny, can you think of any other reasons besides rage that could account for the method of killing?"

"Certainly, but none anywhere near as likely."

"Let me try a couple," I say. "Let's suppose that Mr. Downey had friends, possibly accomplices, that the murderer also had a rather strong disagreement with. Perhaps he was killing Mr. Downey as a way to frighten them. Is it possible that this method of killing would send a stronger message to those people? Might the killer believe that this approach would make them more afraid?"

"Possible, but unlikely," she says.

"Really? The horrible beheadings that we see in the news, conducted by terrorist groups . . . do you not believe those murderers are attempting to send a message? To frighten and intimidate by their brutality?"

"In that case, yes."

"Okay, so now we have another motive besides anger. Let's see if we can come up with another one. Are you aware that there is testimony that Mr. Infante threatened to slit Mr. Downey's throat in the week before the murder?"

"I am, yes."

"If someone else knew that he had made that threat, and that someone wanted to kill Mr. Downey and make it appear as if Mr. Infante committed the crime, wouldn't it make sense for him to slit Mr. Downey's throat?"

"They would have to know the specifics of the threat," she said.

"Of course they would," I agree. "And by that do you mean that the threat might have had to be made in public, like in a crowded bar?"

"I can't speak to that," she says.

"That's fine. So let's sum up. The killer's reason for committing this type of killing could have been either rage, or to send a message, or to frame someone else. Is that your testimony?"

"They are not equal possibilities."

"We're not looking for equal, Dr. Reny. We're looking for reasonable. Can you say beyond a reasonable doubt that the two alternative explanations I provided did not happen in this case?"

I can see her mind racing for an alternative to the obvious, but she's drawing a blank. "I cannot," she says.

"That's okay, no one could. Thank you. No further questions."

There's a message waiting for me on my cell phone from Sam; and it's a welcome piece of positive news.

"I checked into Parelli, the dockworker guy," he says. "He hasn't taken in any unusual amounts of money, just his salary from the government."

"I'm not happy to hear that."

"But I took it a step further and checked his wife's account.

She's had three hundred grand wired into her account in the last eighteen months, and she is unemployed."

"Great job, Sam. Can you find out where the wires are from?"

"I'm checking that now."

"Thanks, Sam," I say.

Pieces are falling into place. Not rapidly enough, but we may be getting somewhere. Our big task remains to show a connection between Downey and Brantley.

We have some evidence to that effect, but that demonstrated connection has to be much stronger to convince Judge Klingman. I have to be able to tie Downey to the world of diamond smuggling, as a way to show the jury that he was involved with very dangerous people who might well have ended his life.

And I may know how to do that.

I reach Agent Hernandez on the first try. This in itself is a surprise; I thought I'd have more trouble. He's made his arrest already, so his need for any information I might provide is therefore considerably less.

"You've got information for me?" is how he starts the conversation. "Is this you being a good citizen?"

"You can read me like a book," I say. "My country 'tis of thee, sweet land of liberty."

"Touching," he says. "Let's hear it."

"The bedrock of our country is sharing."

"I've got nothing for you," he says. "And I doubt very much you have anything for me."

"What about the customs officer who has been knowingly allowing the stuff into the country? And who has been paid three hundred thousand to do so?"

"On the other hand," he says, "who doesn't believe in sharing? It's the bedrock of our country, depending on what is being shared."

"You're a patriot," I say. "Here's what I want. I'm sure you have a good case against Divac. But if you don't even know who they're using in your own department, then you don't have everything, and you must be relying on a witness. I want to know who it is, and I want access to him or her."

"I can't give you that," he says. "It's confidential."

"Bullshit. Even as we speak, the U.S. attorney is turning the name and every statement he made over to Divac's attorney. It's called discovery, and Divac's attorney has no obligation to keep it confidential."

There is a pause, and he says, "I'll get back to you."

"When?"

"When I get back to you. Sit tight."

I barely have time to assume the tight-sitting position when he calls back, obviously having checked with his superiors or the U.S. attorney, and probably both. Again I'm surprised at his level of interest in what I have to say, particularly since his first words are, "You've got a deal." Then he says, "You go first."

"His name is Gino Parelli. He's a supervisor at Port Newark. The payoffs are going to his wife."

"How do you know all this?" he asks.

I won't tell him that; it could come back to bite Sam, who's been doing the illegal hacking. "That I can't share with you. But anything you get from Parelli that can help my case, I want."

Hernandez agrees, so I continue. "Who is the witness against Divac?"

"Guy by the name of Paul Turner. He works for Divac. He was his right-hand man, so he saw everything. If Divac took a shit, Turner wiped his ass."

"I met him. Is he implicated and you turned him?"

"No," he says. "Divac was running a private operation alongside the legit one. He was a loner in it; as far as we can tell none of the other employees were involved. Turner is clean, but he's scared. We've got him protected."

"Tell him I'm coming," I say. "And tell him I won't hurt him."

"And you make sure I'm the first person you go to with any information you get. From anywhere."

"Doesn't sound like you're confident of your case against Divac," I say.

"Divac is history."

I call Sam and ask him if Paul Turner's name came up anywhere on Downey or Brantley's phone records. I don't recall seeing it, but I want to make sure.

"No," Sam says. "First time I've heard the name."

I'm going to contact Turner to set up a meeting, but I'll wait until the morning, in order to give time for Hernandez to tell him to expect me. Dylan is scheduled to wrap up his case in the morning, and then I'll ask the judge to let me start our defense on Monday. That will give me a few days to try to make some headway on this.

If I don't come up with something, the defense case is going to be fairly short.

Paul Turner doesn't sound thrilled to hear from me. Actually, he sounds fairly miserable. He has pissed off some very dangerous people, and at this point he might be regretting that a bit.

I identify myself and ask if he remembers me from our meeting in Divac's office. He says that he does, but that it "seems like a lifetime ago."

"Did Agent Hernandez tell you I was going to call?" I ask.

"He did. He said I should talk to you, which means I guess I have no choice."

"I'm an excellent conversationalist," I say. "You should hear me at cocktail parties. Can I come over now?"

I can almost see him shrug through the phone. "Might as well; I'm not going anywhere."

"Where are you?"

He hesitates for a moment, then says, "I'm in the Crowne Plaza, in the Meadowlands."

"What room?"

"I don't want to say over the phone. Just stand in the lobby; one of my protectors will bring you up to my cell block."

This sounds like one bitter guy.

The Crowne Plaza is only about twenty-five minutes from my house. It's one of a group of quite nice, modern hotels that have opened in the Meadowlands/Secaucus area. The location makes perfect sense; it provides easy access to Manhattan, Newark Airport, and the Meadowlands Sports Complex.

I park the car and walk into the large modern lobby. There's a federal agent there, and I would know that even if he wasn't approaching me. I think all agents share one dark gray suit; they just pass it around to whoever needs it that day.

"Carpenter?" he asks.

"I'm flattered that you recognized me."

"Let's go."

He heads toward the elevator. He doesn't look back to see if I'm following him; I'm quite sure he doesn't care either way. He did his job by coming down here in the first place. But I follow dutifully along, since he is going to bring me to Turner, and that is where I want to be.

We go to the top floor, and when we get out of the elevator, I see another agent in the very long hallway. I continue to follow my personal escort to the room all the way at the end of the hall. He knocks twice, and another agent opens the door.

Compared to this agent, the one who brought me upstairs is Chuckles the Clown. I can see behind him that this is a large suite, and all this guy does is frown and jerk his head toward a room adjacent to what is the living room.

"You guys crack me up," I say, and I head for the closed door of the room he's indicating.

I knock the same double knock that the agent did, and a voice tells me to come in. I open the door, and see that it's the bedroom of the suite, and Turner is sitting on one of two chairs across from the bed.

"Let this be a lesson to you: don't ever do the right thing," he says.

I nod. "Words to live by. But I assume they're not forcing you to be here?"

He frowns. "No, but they told me that if I don't let them protect me, then my life expectancy will be about forty-five minutes."

"Those actuarial tables are really accurate."

"Yeah. Well, I'll do this for a couple of days, and then I'm out of here. I'll disappear, and come back for the trial." He pauses, and then adds, "Maybe."

It's time to cut back on the chitchat. "How long have you known Divac was bad?" I ask.

He shrugs. "Suspected or knew?"

"You pick."

"I've probably suspected for two years, but a kind of denial sets it. When you don't want to know something, it's easy not to know it."

"How did you find out?"

"That doesn't matter," he says.

"So who's running the company now?"

He shrugs. "I have no idea, and to be honest, I couldn't care less."

"So you're not a part of that company any longer?"

"I think you know the answer to that," he says. "Now what was it you wanted to talk to me about?"

"You know about the case I'm trying?" I ask.

He shakes his head. "Not really."

"Tommy Infante is accused of murdering Gerald Downey. Downey was connected to Eric Brantley, which means he was connected to the conspiracy your boss was running. I also know that Downey was involved with bringing smuggled diamonds in through Port Newark, and I know which employee down there was letting the whole thing happen. I've given the information to the customs agents."

"Do I really need to hear all this?" Turner asks. "I've sort of got my own troubles."

"I understand. I've just got a few questions, and then I'll leave you alone. Do you know anything about Gerald Downey? Ever heard of him? Know of any connection between him and Divac?"

"He was a low-level player, did some dirty work, but not much."

"What about Brantley? Where did he fit in?"

"He wasn't a key player. He got the idea in his head that he could bring diamonds into the country illegally. Alan was not about to tolerate the competition, no matter how insignificant it was."

"So Divac had him killed?"

Turner nods. "I believe so, though it's only my opinion. I do know that he had Caruso killed, so I assume the same was true of Brantley."

"And Healy?"

He shrugs. "Healy was Divac's muscle. My guess is he was trying to play both sides, Brantley and Divac. Apparently Divac found some new muscle."

"But you don't know who that is?"

He shakes his head. "I don't. Are we done here?"

I've gotten confirmation of a lot of what I knew, but I still don't have the provable link between Downey and Brantley, at least not enough of a link to base a defense on.

"Pretty much," I say. "But I want you to know that there is a significant chance I'm going to call you to testify."

He actually laughs a short laugh at the prospect. "Testify to what? That I know nothing about your client or his victim?"

"Welcome to my case," I say.

Our archrival is in my kitchen, and he's maybe four feet tall. Yes, when I get home there's Will Rubenstein, starting shortstop for Ricky's Peewee League team, actually sucking down chocolate milk and cookies with Ricky. And Laurie, believe it or not, is serving him.

We have met the enemy, and he is us.

"Andy, come sit down with the boy who is depriving you of the chance to bask in the glory of having a Hall of Fame baseball player for a son" is what Laurie really means when she says, "Andy, come join us. You know Will Rubenstein. . . ."

"Sure, good to see you, Will," I say, taking a seat with them.

"Hi."

"How's baseball coming?"

"Okay" is all he says, obviously smart enough not to reveal too much.

"You ever play right field?" I ask. "You'd be really good at it."

"Nah."

"What about soccer? That's a fun game."

"Nah."

Laurie is staring daggers at me, so I pretend to be friendly for a few more minutes, and then head for the den to do some work.

I've got Dylan's last witnesses to prepare for, but then more importantly, I've got to figure out a way to get Judge Klingman to allow me to introduce testimony about Gerald Downey's connection to Brantley, Divac, and the world of diamond smuggling.

I still don't have enough evidence of a link to have a chance of getting it in. It's crucial that I come up with a strategy to overcome this, for one very important reason: jurors want to have someone to blame for the crime. The chance of them acquitting Tommy goes way up if they can point to someone else as the possible killer.

To be able to associate Downey with the dangerous people in the smuggling world, and to be able to point to all these other murders that have taken place, would go a long way toward providing this jury with the reasonable doubt that we need. But to get there, we have to get by the judge.

I bounce back and forth on this, according to my own self-interest, but I think that the admissibility standard is too strict. My basic philosophy is let the lawyer bring it in, and then let the jury decide if it's relevant and meaningful to the case. If they think the lawyer is fishing, or bringing in unrelated issues, then they can decide he or she is a dope and punish the client for it.

Bottom line, as it relates to Tommy's case, is that I think this jury should be able to know things like the fact that Downey has been hanging around with vicious killers.

We would all be much better off in a world ruled by Judge Andy Carpenter.

It's a little hard for me to concentrate on the end of Dylan's case. I'm already focused on our own, and Dylan's last witnesses are of little significance. They are basically two more forensics people and Downey's prom queen landlady, whom Laurie and I spoke with.

But I need to be prepared for all eventualities, so I go over the technical reports that the forensics people prepared. They are not going to say anything that hasn't been said already; if Dylan has a weakness as a prosecutor, it is the fact that he beats facts to death. The jury has heard it all, and they're tired, and Dylan making them sit through more of the same has got to be annoying.

Downey's landlady, Helen Streiter, is another case in point. Reading the transcript of her interview with the prosecutors, it's clear that she has nothing substantive to offer. Basically, she is going to say that Downey and Tommy knew each other, and that she had seen Tommy go to Downey's house.

If anything, that will cut in our favor. We haven't denied that they knew each other, and Tommy's fingerprints in the house demonstrate that he had been there. Streiter will be providing us with the chance to again mention that the prints could have been left at another time, not necessarily when the murder took place.

She'll also say some other stuff that will work in Dylan's favor, but nothing we can't handle.

As I go over the documents relating to her testimony, I find my mind wandering. This is not exactly a rare event; the difference is that this time it's wandering in a direction that will actually be helpful.

I check the witness list that Dylan submitted at the beginning of the trial. Some of them are not going to be called, or at least Dylan isn't planning to call them. I'm hoping to change his mind.

My plan is forming. Helen Streiter doesn't know it, but she's going to start the ball rolling toward convincing Judge Klingman to admit all the testimony I want.

Maybe.

If all goes well.

I hope.

The FBI was called in to execute the arrest of Gino Parelli. It was therefore their call where to do so, and they opted for his home, rather than Port Newark, where he worked. Part of this was in deference to their sister agency. To do so in public, at the pier, might have resulted in unnecessary publicity and embarrassment for the customs people, as it was one of their own who had turned bad.

The agents had no reason to expect any trouble. The reports were that Parelli had spent a normal day at work, and did not seem stressed or anxious. No one detected any unusual behavior, and there was no reason to believe that he was in any way aware that he was about to go down.

The negative, of course, was that Parelli's wife was likely present. There was no way to know for sure, and no way around it if she was. The arrest was not about to be delayed to protect her sensibilities.

The Parellis lived in a modest home in Lyndhurst, New Jersey. They were on a cul-de-sac, which in and of itself carried both positives and negatives. Being very quiet and barely trafficked, the agents' arrival would certainly be noticed. But the position of the house on the end of the street would make escape even more impossible than it would otherwise have been.

None of the agents were particularly worried. They approached their job with care and precision, and prepared for all eventualities. But it was likely to be a routine arrest; Parelli would go quietly.

The agents arrived in force, ten of them in four cars. Two of them went to the front door, two went to each side of the house, and two went to the back. The remaining two agents stood in front, behind the two at the door, providing backup.

It was Special Agent Otis Masters who rang the bell three times, getting no response each time. Through the door he could hear sound coming from what appeared to be a television. He recognized it as one of the cooking shows his wife watched on a regular basis, even though she couldn't so much as successfully boil an egg.

They were armed with a search warrant, so had no concerns about entering the house. Masters and his partner thought it would be unnecessary and overly dramatic to break down the door, so instead Masters picked the lock, a process that took all of five seconds.

Masters then turned the knob and was the first to enter, which meant he was the first to see the blood.

There actually wasn't that much of it; Mr. and Mrs. Parelli each had neat little bullet holes in the center of their foreheads. They had seen the shooter, but were in no condition to reveal his identity. That, they would take to their graves.

The agents sprung into action, professionally locking down the house and the surrounding area. A full-scale search was conducted, but the killer had long since departed.

For the FBI, the evening had not gone as planned.

Hike tells me about the deaths of Gino Parelli and his wife. I didn't listen to the radio on the way to court; I was too intent on going over my approach for the cross-examination of Helen Streiter. If I play it right, she is going to open the door for me to get all the testimony I want admitted.

I would be lying if I said that I am crushed to hear the news. I certainly did not want Parelli dead, nor do I think that was a fair punishment for his crimes. But he knowingly dealt with very dangerous people, and committed illegal acts alongside them. He either knew the risks, or should have. The greater tragedy was that his wife had to suffer the same fate.

I imagine the deaths are being greeted with considerable consternation in the Customs Bureau and FBI. The only people who would have known the arrest was taking place were the people in those agencies, and there must be a real worry that there is an informant among them.

I feel relieved that I had not mentioned Parelli's name to anyone other than Laurie and Sam. Sam may have included Hilda and Eli Mandlebaum in the secret, since they retrieved online information about him. But the chance that they are criminal informants is about as likely as the chance that I am secretly a waitress at Hooters. The leak did not come from the Carpenter camp.

I hadn't gotten a chance to tell Hike my plan for getting the diamond smuggling testimony admitted. I do so now, and when I finish, he says, "Interesting. I give it maybe a twenty percent chance."

Coming from Hike, that is a slam dunk, so I'm feeling pretty good about it.

In any event, I have to put all of it out of my mind now, because Dylan starts the session by calling Helen Streiter. The last time I saw her she was in a housedress and barefoot; this time she is dressed much more presentably, in a skirt and blouse, with a jacket. I have no doubt that Dylan told her exactly what to wear; I wouldn't be surprised if he bought the outfit for her. He should have told her to wear less makeup: she's piled it on way too thick.

Dylan begins by having her identify her connection to Downey; she was his landlady. He lived in the building that her late husband had bought before they were married, and was one of three buildings left to her in his will.

"How well did you know Mr. Downey?" he asks.

"I knew him; I talked to him some. He paid his rent on time."

It's a beautiful tribute to the departed Gerry Downey; by now I doubt there's a dry eye in the courtroom.

Dylan asks if she has ever seen Tommy Infante before today, and she says yes, that she had seen him visit Downey on at least three occasions. It's what I was hoping she'd say, and what I knew she'd say.

Under Dylan's questioning, she goes on to describe an argument she heard the two men having, a few weeks before the murder. She couldn't hear exactly what they were saying, but they were both very angry, and she thinks it was about money.

Everything goes smoothly; she has clearly been rehearsed. It's all as it was in the discovery documents, and as I hoped and expected. Her key comment, the one that will allow me to ask the questions I'm going to ask, was in saying that she saw Tommy visit Downey on a number of occasions.

What I am going to need to do in the defense case is introduce the fact that Downey associated with dangerous and unsavory people. It is, in a way, negative character testimony. But I can't introduce it without legal provocation; Klingman would never see it as relevant and allow it. The only way I can do it is as rebuttal testimony, which means I need Dylan's help. And Helen Streiter's.

My first question is, "Ms. Streiter, you said that you heard Mr. Downey and Mr. Infante arguing. Is that correct?"

"Yes."

"And that they were very angry?"

"Yes."

"How long was it until the police came?" It's the same question I asked the bartender after Tommy threatened Downey in the bar, and I get the same answer.

"They didn't come."

"You didn't call them?" I ask, feigning surprise.

"Why would I call them?" she asks.

"So you, and your other neighbors, weren't afraid it would become violent?"

"I didn't call them," she says, not answering the question, which is fine with me.

"Where were you when you heard the argument?"

"Sitting on my front porch; it was warm out."

"You sit there a lot?" I ask.

"I guess so; when it's warm."

"So you can see people coming and going to Mr. Downey's house?"

"That's not why I sat there."

"I understand that," I say. "You sat there because it is warm in the spring and summer. Is Mr. Infante the only visitor you ever saw Mr. Downey have?"

"No, there were quite a few."

I then proceed to take Streiter through a list of the people she mentioned in her interview with the police. It is not exactly a Who's Who of Academia and Philanthropy, and in each case I introduce evidence describing some of the transgressions of the visitors, two of whom are in jail.

I am able to do this because Dylan introduced the subject of visitors that Streiter saw come to the house. It doesn't give me the okay to bring in other unsavory characters, like the diamond smugglers, because Dylan didn't go there.

I've led the horse's ass to water; all I can do now is wait to see if he drinks.

Dylan doesn't have to rehabilitate Gerald Downey's character. Downey is the victim here; it doesn't matter to the law if he was a Boy Scout or not. The state of New Jersey frowns on murder, even when the person murdered has not surrounded himself with choir boys.

My hope is that Dylan's pride and competitiveness will come into play. He is probably irritated with himself for calling Helen Streiter; she was not necessary to his case, and her testimony about Tommy visiting Downey opened the door for me to bring in the other people who visited as well.

Now, because of that slight mistake, he may feel the need to compensate for it, to mitigate or remove the damage. If he does, then the door he will open will be as wide as the Lincoln Tunnel.

A promising sign is that Dylan asked for an early lunch break, so he could line up his witnesses. If he were just going to wrap up the case with the forensic stuff, I wouldn't think he'd have to scramble like this.

When court reconvenes, Dylan calls Sue Pyles, the director of a facility in downtown Paterson called It Feels Like Home. It's a place where kids go after school and on weekends. They have a basketball court, books, pool, table tennis, and various other activities designed to keep kids off the street.

I'm familiar with the place, and Laurie and I have taught some literacy programs there, as well as donating money. Sue is a terrific, dedicated lady, has been doing this for thirty years, and is no doubt responsible for improving the life of many hundreds of kids.

At Dylan's prodding, Sue talks about Gerald Downey, starting from the time he was a teenager and a regular at the facility.

"Did he return there as an adult?" he asks.

"Oh, yes. Many times. He would play basketball and Ping-Pong with the kids. They saw him as their friend, and he was. Gerald was very helpful to us; he really cared about the young people."

She cites some examples of good work that Downey had done at the center, and specific examples of him helping certain kids. I have to admit I'm impressed and surprised. I never met Downey, but what I knew of him did not include this kind of positive assessment.

In Dylan's typical style, he keeps Sue on the stand too long, going over the same ground at least three times. By the time it's my turn, it's hard to believe that anyone is still awake, which is okay, since I have no intention of doing anything dramatic.

"Ms. Pyles, do you have any information that directly relates to this case?"

"Not really; just what I've read."

"Do you consider yourself very well informed on what Gerald Downey's life was like when he was not at your center?"

"I wouldn't say so, no."

"So it's fair to say that you are here to testify to what you consider Gerald Downey's good character?"

She nods. "Yes."

"You've described his interactions with other people, also not related to this case, as an example of that good character?"

"I have."

"Thank you for coming here, and thank you for the great work that you do," I say. "No further questions."

I steal a quick look at Dylan, who is looking straight ahead, an impassive look on his face. He's a smart guy; he has to know what just happened.

If Vegas were handicapping this trial, he'd still be a big favorite. But Dylan and I both know that the odds just got a bit shorter.

When trying a murder case, it's easy to get lost in the weeds. A lawyer in a case like this must have a complete command of the facts, down to the smallest minutiae. Not to know a fact, or not be able to recall it immediately, could mean a key moment is lost, and a trial can accurately be described as a series of key moments.

But that kind of mind-set tends to obscure the big picture, and yet the real answers are almost always found there. At various points in any trial, I try to sit down for an hour or so, clear my mind, and focus on the larger issues.

I usually do this with someone, since talking out loud and having an interplay help to crystallize the issues. My choices are always Laurie or Hike, which is the definition of a no-brainer. Laurie is smart and a pleasure to be with; Hike is smart and absolute torture to be with.

Hmmm . . . what to do . . . what to do . . .

Tonight I choose Laurie, which if my count is correct, is the 144th consecutive time I've done so. She pours us both a glass of wine, and we sit in the den, with a U2 CD on in the background.

"Here's something I don't understand" is how I start. "Our

theory is that Eric Brantley went overseas, was introduced in some fashion to diamond smugglers, and decided to get into it himself. Right so far?"

"Right so far," she says.

"So they give him the name of Gerald Downey, who was involved in the process, but clearly not a key player. At best he was a low-level soldier, elevated slightly because he knew Parelli, and was therefore able to help get the stuff past customs."

"And Downey introduced Brantley to at least some of the members of the conspiracy," she says.

I nod. "Right. But what I'm wondering is what the hell made Brantley so important? Why did his arrival on the scene cause this commotion? Why was he significant enough to warrant killing him, Caruso, Downey, and setting Tommy up? And I haven't even mentioned Brantley's boss, Professor Horowitz. Tommy is sure he's dead as well."

"He was a threat to them, a competitor. When there is that much money at stake, competition isn't welcomed."

"What kind of competition could he have been? He was a novice, with no money, and one pathetic connection to a nobody like Gerald Downey. They could have told Downey to tell him to get lost, or even threaten him if he didn't."

"But they treated him seriously," she says. "Beyond seriously."

I nod. "That's for sure. I also can't figure out why Brantley got into it. As far as I can tell, his life wasn't about going for the money, or doing anything criminal, or dangerous. So somebody mentions diamond smuggling to him and he jumps in with both feet. It makes no sense to me."

"Maybe he never had a chance at this kind of money," she says. "And unfortunately, the only one left alive who would be able to explain it is Divac, and he's sitting in a jail cell. So he's not going to be talking to anyone, unless he pleads. And they wouldn't let him plead to anything but life, so he has no incentive."

"But I don't think it ends with him," I say. "The customs agent, Hernandez, was very anxious to get information from me. At this stage, Divac is in the U.S. prosecutor's hands, and the agents should be moving on. They either don't have a strong case against Divac, or it goes deeper than him."

"What exactly was Divac doing?"

"You mean allegedly doing?"

She smiles. "Yes, I mean allegedly." As an ex-cop, Laurie is quicker than I am to assign guilt.

"Well, as I understand it from Hernandez, the illegal diamonds come in without certification or identification as legit. Divac, who dealt in legal diamonds as well, was able to provide all of that, which made them infinitely more valuable. So Divac was buying illegal diamonds at a reduced price, and then marking them up after he certified them."

"And the people he paid in the first place?"

"They apparently use the money to buy weapons, for whatever part of the world they happen to be fighting in. That reminds me . . . ," I start to say.

"What?"

"When Cindy first called me, to ask me to deal with the customs guys, she told me lives were at stake."

"Weapons have a tendency to kill people."

I nod. "But my sense was that the people were not in some far-off war zone. My sense was that it was closer to home."

"You could ask her."

"I will. But I want to wait until I know exactly what questions to ask, and until I have something to trade."

"And until then?"

"Until then I defend Tommy. I try to get the judge to admit my evidence, and then I try to get the jury to buy it."

"What are your chances?" she asks.

"Pretty good on the first part. Pretty bad on the second."

Dylan went nuts when he saw our witness list. That's actually a supposition of mine, since I wasn't actually there when he saw the list. We had sent it to his office as part of the normal course of business. But it makes me feel better to imagine him upset, so that's my story and I'm sticking to it.

My speculation is given substantial credibility by the motion he has filed in response. It's peppered with words like "fishing expedition" and "irrelevant," with a few "mockery"s thrown in. It borders on the legal equivalent of a meltdown.

Hike writes a brief in response to Dylan's, and we submit it to the court. Judge Klingman then calls a special session out of the presence of the jury, so that we can fight it out.

I'm feeling pretty good about our chances, and very good about the opportunity to rub Dylan's nose in his mistake. Putting a damper on my enthusiasm is the knowledge that if we lose, so does Tommy. At this point he is likely going down even if we can present our full case; if we can't he's going down very, very hard.

Judge Klingman is walking toward his seat on the bench, and we rise on command of the bailiff. As we do so, Tommy whispers to me, "This is important, huh?"

"This is important," I say.

"I've read the briefs," Judge Klingman says. "Let's hear some oral arguments. Let me rephrase that: Let's hear some brief oral arguments. Mr. Campbell?"

"Your Honor, the witness list that the defense has offered would be a source of amusement if this were not such a serious matter. It quite literally could be a list for another case entirely, filed in this matter by mistake. I daresay it would be just as appropriate, or more correctly inappropriate, for any case on Your Honor's docket."

He blathers on about this for a few more minutes, and after the fourth repetition of the same thing, Judge Klingman stops him and says, "Mr. Carpenter?"

"Your Honor, I'm frankly puzzled" is how I start. I almost never use the word "frankly." When a politician uses it, it signals two things: that he's definitely lying, and that he's admitted he's not frank in his other statements.

But it seems appropriate here, because everybody knows that I'm lying, that I'm not really puzzled. I continue, "As we pointed out in our brief, our intention is to educate the jury as to Mr. Downey's associations and relationships. We are simply continuing the process that Mr. Campbell saw fit to begin. He seems to be saying it is proper for the prosecution, but not for the defense. I don't understand that. Frankly, I don't."

Dylan jumps in. "I did not begin the process of calling irrelevant witnesses. Ms. Streiter had evidence that was germane to this case."

"Your Honor," I say, "I would invite the court to review the transcript in the unlikely event that I am remembering this incorrectly. Mr. Campbell had Ms. Streiter here to testify about a visitor, Mr. Infante, to Mr. Downey's house. I then questioned her about other visitors."

"Which was itself improper," Dylan says.

"I don't recall you objecting," Judge Klingman points out.

"It was insignificant testimony; I didn't want to waste the court's time." He didn't use the word "frankly" in that sentence, but it would have fit perfectly. And the other interesting thing about "frankly" is that it can go almost anywhere. He could have said, "Frankly, it was insignificant testimony." Or, "It was frankly insignificant testimony." Or, "I frankly didn't want to waste the court's time."

"And I for one appreciate that," I say. "Though I was somewhat surprised when Mr. Campbell used a considerable amount of the court's time later that afternoon, when he questioned Ms. Pyles about Mr. Downey's charitable work. It seemed to have nothing to do with the case itself; Ms. Pyles admitted as much when I asked her."

"That was in response to the defense's questioning of Ms. Streiter."

Time to move in for the kill. "So you're saying I opened the door? That's your position? Your Honor, it was Mr. Campbell who opened the door; he blew a hole in it. When we arrived the door had been entirely removed, and hot air was blowing in."

Dylan is getting angrier by the moment, but keeping himself under control. "Your Honor, the bottom line is that the defense is trying to litigate another matter entirely. We are here to determine the guilt or innocence of this defendant for this crime, and Mr. Carpenter is trying to deflect the attention of the court to something completely different and unrelated."

My turn. "Your Honor, since we're now talking about 'bottom lines,' here's how I see it. Mr. Campbell questioned Ms. Streiter about Mr. Downey's visitors, so we did the same. Then he brought in a witness not related to this case. We could do the same, but we're respecting the court, and our view is they are related to this case. But at its core we are mirroring Mr. Campbell's actions. Yet instead of being flattered, he's upset. As I may have mentioned before, I'm frankly puzzled."

Judge Klingman says, "Yes, I believe you may have mentioned that. Mr. Carpenter, I am going to allow the contested testimony, within reason. If it becomes redundant, or goes too far afield, I'm going to rein you in. Mr. Campbell, I don't find any question at all that you in fact opened the door for this testimony. See you tomorrow, gentlemen."

Alek was not going to meet them at some cave or campsite. That was once his life, and it molded him into the man he had become. But that was well behind him; he had earned his money, he was earning it still, and he had come to require more creature comfort. He made no apologies for it; in fact, Alek never remembered apologizing for anything in his entire life.

Not that this meeting was being held in lavish surroundings. The diner in Caribou, Maine, was not exactly a five-star restaurant, though their coffee tasted better. But this was the best that could be arranged under the circumstances, so it would have to do.

There were three of them, all males, and Alek didn't ask their names, nor did they offer them. Their names were unimportant, as were they. Alek knew that they might as well have been called Pawn I, Pawn II, and Pawn III, because that's what they were.

Three doomed pawns.

They were on a mission that would end in their deaths. They were fine with that; it would further their cause in a way that nothing else had. The Boston Marathon bombers had tried to punish America for what they saw as its frequent illegal occupation of their Middle Eastern lands. This would make the point far more clearly and forcefully; the tables would be turned and Americans would finally know what it was like to be victims of ruthless occupiers.

But Alek had even less interest in their cause than their names. He briefly flirted with the idea of not providing the arms at all, of reneging on their deal once he had his money, and leaving them to wait at their campsites until they gave up and went home. But he rejected that idea, because to fail to deliver would impact his future business. More importantly, he rejected it because those who were financing these people were serious and dangerous people. No need to make more enemies than necessary.

Alek drank coffee while they drank tea. It seemed a delicate drink for soon-to-be murderers and suicide victims, but to each his last taste. "Describe your mission," he instructed them.

"Why do you need to know this?" Pawn I asked, warily.

The truth was that Alek did not need to know it; he didn't even much care what their mission was. Ordinarily he wouldn't even have asked the question, but this was not an ordinary situation.

The Americans did not get overly upset by arms trading in general, so long as those arms were to be used in places where there were no Americans, and little American interest. But this was very different; these were to be used against Americans, on American soil.

The U.S. government would come after all involved, and though Alek was confident he could avoid scrutiny and any negative consequences, he still wanted to know what he was dealing with. He also considered the possibility of getting back some of his merchandise. After this was over, these saps would be dead, but at least some of the arms themselves would live on.

"It is always a part of my contract," Alek lied. "I have no interest in interfering, but I must know what is going to take place."

"We are going to capture an American town. It is a small island, but attached to the mainland by a small bridge," Pawn I said. "It will be easy to defend, and easy to destroy."

Pawn II said, with considerably more passion, "They will learn what it is like to have a deadly aggressor on their soil. As we have learned it from them so many times."

Alek didn't even know what country Pawn II was from, and it was of little concern to him. Politics, even geopolitics, interested him only in its ability to provide profit.

But he already knew where the "invasion" was to take place, since that was where the arms were to be delivered. "Ashby," he said.

Pawn I nodded. "Correct."

"And what are your plans once you come ashore?"

"To take complete control."

"And when they come after you?" Alek asked.

"Then we will die defending our territory, as will the people of Ashby."

Pawn III smiled, and spoke in a voice distinctly American. "Or maybe no one will care, and we'll live happily ever after in Ashby."

Alek had suspected that there were Americans involved in the operation; they were prized recruits for zealots like this. "Okay," he said, "once I receive the money, I will get word to you to move in. You know where the boats are going to be?"

Pawn I nodded. "We do. Our main concern is timing."

"It will be soon," Alek said, and smiled. "Very soon."

Laurie and I share many attitudes, viewpoints, and preferences. I'm not talking about run-of-the-mill issues like human values, dignity, and the desire to make the world a better place. That's really her thing.

I'm talking about real-life stuff that people deal with every day, like what kind of movies to watch. Those are the kinds of things on which real relationships succeed or fail.

She and I are on the same page when it comes to movies; in fact, we're on the same two pages. Not only do we like the same films, but we like to see them over and over.

At any one time, our television guide offers close to 12 million movies, or at least it seems that way. We haven't seen about 11,997,000 of them, yet as we scroll through, we always settle on one of a handful that we've seen repeatedly and love.

I'm not necessarily talking about particular types of films; they could be dramas or comedies, high quality or low. But for some reason we find them comfortable; when we see they're on, we can pick them up at any point and just relax and enjoy.

I've just finished spending four hours going over the case files, and when I go up to bed, Laurie is watching one of those movies. It's called *The Freshman,* and stars Marlon Brando and

Matthew Broderick. It's a comedy in which the teenage Broderick's life gets comically turned upside down when he meets Brando, reprising his Mafia chieftain role from *The Godfather.*

When I come in, Laurie is sitting up in bed, eating popcorn. "You okay with watching for a while?" she asks, knowing I have to be up early in the morning.

"Absolutely," I say, and take my place close to her, so I can grab some of the popcorn.

It's early in the film, and Broderick is just learning who the Brando character is, and the kind of power he possesses. He comes to Brando's home, and is greeted at the door by his daughter, who lets him in.

Sitting above the fireplace is a replica of the *Mona Lisa,* except the daughter casually informs Broderick that it's not a replica at all, but rather the real thing. It had been stolen, she says, and the painting hanging in the Louvre is the copy.

Overall, it's a very funny scene, but I'm not laughing. Instead I'm dialing the phone, calling Sam Willis. It's eleven-thirty at night, but as always he answers on the first ring.

"Talk to me," he says, alert and as if he were waiting for my call.

"Sam, I know it's late, but can you come over here?"

"What's up?"

"I need you to help me google."

"What's that?"

"I need help googling something."

"Are you serious? Any moron can google. I can teach you over the phone. Laurie can teach you. Ricky can teach you. I bet Tara can teach you."

"Sam, I can google. But I need to do a really in-depth search, and you can get to more places than I can."

He agrees to come over, and arrives within fifteen minutes. I use the time to tell Laurie what I'm looking for, and I have to admit I'm relieved when she doesn't laugh at me.

I start Sam off by asking him to search for a particular article I read, maybe a year ago. I don't know where or when I saw it, and I can only describe it in basic terms. Of course, Sam finds it in about twenty seconds. Once he does, it gives him some other terms to search for. The information starts to pour out; I have a laser printer, but it can't keep up.

I won't say that Sam finishes what he's doing; there is so much information available that he effectively could continue and never finish. But after about an hour, we decide that we have enough, and we take the next hour to read through what we have.

It doesn't confirm my theory; it's not possible for it to have done that. But it does confirm that it is possible, and that is all I hoped it would do.

I no longer believe that Eric Brantley was involved with smuggling diamonds into the country.

I believe he was creating them.

The article and others like it talk about copying valuable treasures. Huge strides have been made in artificially duplicating works of art, primarily through 3-D printing. I don't begin to understand it, and I don't have to; it's enough to know that things like this exist.

Less advanced, but getting there, is the ability of scientists to artificially produce diamonds. There are a number of processes to do so, the most promising of which is something called chemical vapor deposition. I have taken and sat through many depositions in my career, but none of the chemical vapor variety.

To this point, the created diamonds are very close to the real thing, and certainly beyond the ability of consumers to tell the difference. But they're not exact; among other things they're not quite as hard, and experts using their examining equipment can usually detect the fakes.

But everyone seems to acknowledge that perfect duplications are only a matter of time, and certainly in both art and precious stones, the implications are enormous.

How many wealthy people will be willing to pay huge sums to have Picassos hanging on their walls if both they and their guests have no idea if they are real or not? Will anyone buy an enormously expensive diamond, if they have no way of knowing if it's fake?

Certainly, many people spend crazy money to buy these rocks because they consider them beautiful. But I would guess that just as many, and maybe more, buy them to impress others. Will they keep buying them if the people they're trying to impress doubt that they are real? And what about their investment value? How much is a precious stone worth if it might not even be precious?

I'm going to need some time to digest what this might mean for our case, and for the situation Eric Brantley must have been in. He was by all accounts a brilliant chemist, and I'm assuming that he and his partner, Caruso, perfected the process, and did so in secret. But he must have decided there was much more money in the real stones than the fake ones, so he tried to bring his creations to market as real.

Doing so was fraud, a criminal act, so he tried to align himself with the criminals that were already trading in illegal stones. It was naïve of him, but clearly would have provided him with the best chance to make huge amounts of money from his discovery.

But how would his new associates have viewed Brantley's entry on the scene, with his newly created diamonds? They could have reacted in one of two ways. They might have seen it as a huge plus, providing an unending supply of perfect diamonds without the need to pay for them.

But the more farsighted among them could have seen it as a poison pill. They would have reasoned that the truth would eventually come out, and their lifeblood, diamonds, would be devalued forever.

"It fits," Laurie says. "It might have created a war of sorts. Maybe one side wanted to work with Brantley, and the other didn't. When they couldn't work it out, a lot of people paid with their lives."

There's no way to know if we're right about this, but if we are, it explains a lot. "This is why Brantley created such a stir," I say. "I couldn't figure out why a newcomer with no money and no contacts would have been treated with such importance. This makes that understandable."

She nods. "It also would explain why the stones that Downey had were not registered. Brantley had created them, and used them to pay Downey to steal Zoe from us."

"Right. And I think the equipment stolen from the college was what was taken from that barn in Maine. It had to have been the equipment used to make the diamonds."

"I think you've got this one right, Andy."

I'm pleased that I've come up with this theory; like Laurie, I instinctively feel that it's right. But unfortunately, my enthusiasm is somewhat tempered by the reality staring me in the face.

"This would be good news if we could prove it, which we can't," I say. "And it would be great news if our goal was to solve a smuggling case. But I don't see how it does anything for Tommy Infante."

Willie Miller is the first witness I call in the defense case. It's the riskiest way to begin, akin to a seven-year-old Wallenda kid choosing the Grand Canyon for his first tightrope walk, rather than a two-foot-high wire in the backyard. Willie doesn't have the same filters and verbal safeguards as the rest of us do; he is likely to say anything at any time.

The only saving grace is that he wasn't born with the "lying gene" that so many of us have been blessed with, so whatever does come flying out of his mouth is going to be the truth as he understands it. And the truth is all I want from him now.

In any event, I have no choice but to take the risk. I can't question myself, so I need Willie to testify to the theft of Zoe by Gerald Downey, since that is the first step in tying Downey to Brantley and the carnage that has been the diamond smuggling side of this case.

I start by having Willie give some of his own background, including his seven-year wrongful imprisonment on a murder charge. Dylan will only bring it up anyway, and he'll make it sound sinister, as if perhaps Willie really was guilty. But I didn't get him off on a technicality; he was innocent, and we found the real killer.

Once that has been accomplished, we move on to Willie's partnership with me in the Tara Foundation. He talks about what we do and how we do it, and I can see the dog-loving members of the jury nod their heads in appreciation and approval.

"How many dogs are in the building at any one time?" I ask.

"We have room for twenty-five, so that's how many we always have," he says. "As soon as we find a home for one of them, we rescue another to take its place."

I ask Willie if he telephoned me on the evening of Downey's murder, and he says that he did. He says, "Because the burglar alarm at the foundation went off, and when I got down there I saw that Cheyenne had been stolen."

"Cheyenne is a name that we had given her because we didn't know her real name?" I ask.

He nods. "Right."

I introduce the surveillance camera tape as evidence, which shows the thief entering the building. His sweatshirt is pulled up, covering his face, but anyone can clearly see that the word SYRACUSE is emblazoned on it. The jurors know from the murder scene pictures that Downey was wearing a sweatshirt just like it when he was killed.

"And you knew which dog was stolen?" I ask.

"Of course. It was Cheyenne."

He describes how we followed the GPS device in Cheyenne's collar to Downey's house, and he heard her bark, even though no one came to the door.

"What did you do?"

"Well, Pete was there, and—"

"You mean Captain Stanton of the Paterson Police?"

He nods. "Yeah. Pete. So the three of us went in, and you found Cheyenne, next to Downey's body."

"Had you ever seen Mr. Downey before that?"

"Yeah, he had come in looking to adopt a dog."

"Did he adopt one?" I ask.

"No, I threw him out."

"Why?"

"He said the dog would sleep in a doghouse. That ain't happening," he says, as most of the jury smile their approval.

I lead him through the remaining events of the day of the murder, and he is an excellent witness. He only answers the questions that I ask, and does so concisely, sometimes colorfully. I can only hope he'll get through cross-examination the same way.

It turns out that I don't seem to have anything to worry about. Dylan starts with, "Mr. Miller, did you see the murderer when you were at Mr. Downey's house?"

"No. If I did, he'd be sitting over there instead of Tommy Infante." Willie points to the defense table in case Dylan was unsure what "over there" meant.

Dylan objects to Willie's answer, and seems irritated by the laughter of pretty much everyone in the courtroom. Judge Klingman sustains the objection, and tells the jury to disregard the answer. Good luck with that.

"It's a yes-or-no question, Mr. Miller. Did you see the murderer, or had he left already?"

"I didn't see him," says Willie.

"Thank you. No further questions."

Dylan has actually played it smart. Willie didn't say anything that the jury didn't know already, so Dylan had no reason to have to challenge him. He knows that Willie can be a loose cannon, so there was no upside to giving that cannon a chance to go off.

Willie looks disappointed when Judge Klingman tells him that he can leave the witness stand. He's having fun.

That makes one of us.

Stuart Fowler said a silent thank-you when he saw the rest area. The thank-you was because he couldn't remember the last time he had to go to the bathroom quite that badly. He should have gone at the restaurant, especially after he had two beers, two diet sodas, some water, and a cup of coffee. But he didn't, and he'd been regretting it ever since he got in the car.

The reason the thank-you was silent was that the woman he'd had dinner with, Marti Laird, was sitting in the passenger seat. It was only their third date and he liked her a lot, but their relationship didn't seem quite advanced enough for him to verbally agonize over having to go to the bathroom.

So when they saw the sign for the rest area on the Palisades Parkway, Stuart casually said, "I'm going to stop here, if you don't mind." He said that even though he would have stopped anyway, even if she did mind. Better he should overrule her on that, than piss in the car.

But Marti said, "Sure. No problem," as he knew she would. So he pulled in and parked in the lot. It was fairly dark, so he said, "I'm going to lock the door," and she didn't try to dissuade him from doing so.

Once that was accomplished, Stuart walked toward the building that he knew would contain the restroom. When he got there, he was stunned to see a sign on the door that apologized for the fact that the restroom was closed. Disbelieving, he tried the door, but it was locked.

There was no way Stuart was getting back in that car without relieving himself, so he casually walked along the building, in the direction heading away from Marti and the car. He acted as if he were looking for another entrance, which is what he wanted her to think, if she could see him in the dim light.

But there was no other entrance, and Stuart did not expect there to be one. He was heading for the back of the building, to do his business in the brush and then continue the ride home. There was nothing wrong with what he was doing; he just felt uncomfortable with Marti knowing it.

When he was finished and feeling much, much better, he continued along the back of the building, so as to come out the other side, where the car was.

He was five feet from the end of the building and still zipping up when, in the near darkness, he tripped over the body of Professor Charles Horowitz.

Y ou still want the report on Horowitz, right?"
Sam asks.

It seems a strange question, or maybe I just think it's strange because he's woken me at seven a.m. to ask it. "Of course," I say. "Why?"

"You didn't hear? He's dead. They found his body in a rest area on the Palisades."

Court is not starting until after lunch today because one of the jurors has a doctor's appointment, so I ask Sam to come right over. In the meantime, I turn on the news to see what details of Horowitz's death they might be reporting, but there isn't much.

"Horowitz was a pretty boring guy," Sam says to Laurie and me. "Didn't go out much, and was actually in a bowling league on Tuesday nights. No unusual financial dealings that I can see."

"Tell me something I can use," I say.

"I was getting to that. Three days before he disappeared, he made a phone call to Alan Divac."

"Where? At his home? Cell phone?"

Sam shakes his head. "No. At his company. But on Divac's

private line. I have no way of knowing if he actually talked to Divac."

"Would anyone else have access to that line?"

Sam shrugs. "Can't tell you that either."

"Turner would know," Laurie says to me. "You could ask him."

"I will when I see him."

"When will that be?" she asks.

"Day after tomorrow. I had Hike serve him with a subpoena to testify."

Sam leaves and I place a call to the coroner's office. I'm put right through to Janet Carlson. "Andy, hope I didn't hurt your case with my testimony."

"You were fair," I say, which is true. "But now you have a chance to help my case."

"How?"

"I assume Charles Horowitz was brought to your place last night?"

"He was," she confirms.

"Have you sliced him up yet?" I ask.

"You mean have I performed a medical autopsy on him?"

"Exactly."

"I have not," she says. "I'll be starting in about a half hour."

"Any idea at this point as to cause of death?"

"It's a puzzler," she says. "But based on my years of experience, I have a feeling that the bullet hole in the back of his head could be a factor."

"You're a savvy veteran," I say. "But I have one more question, which I would categorize as the key one. Can you estimate time of death? Within a day or two?"

"Day or two?" she asks, clearly surprised. "He was only dead a couple of hours at the most when they found him."

I thank her and tell Laurie what she said. Then, "They kidnapped him and kept him alive for more than a week."

"Were there ransom demands of any kind?" she asks.

"I don't know, but I would certainly doubt it. I think they needed him, and now they don't need him anymore."

"Needed him for what?"

"He was a chemist, and close to Brantley and Caruso. I think he was their partner, and I think they showed him what they knew."

"So Horowitz was making them diamonds? Then why kill him? Why not keep him around to make more?"

"Maybe they have all they need."

"For what?"

"I don't know the answer to that. But one way or another, I've got a feeling we're going to know soon."

Stephanie Manning is clearly nervous, which isn't really a problem. She's certainly never testified in a murder trial before, so I think the jury will be understanding of her anxiety, and probably sympathetic to it. She's also suffered a loss, which will increase that potential sympathy. It will also probably cause Dylan to go easy on her.

But basically her testimony will be straightforward and pretty hard to screw up, so I think she'll do fine, regardless of her stress level.

"Stephanie, you were close friends with Eric Brantley, is that correct?"

"Yes. He was my boyfriend." Then she uses the same description she had used when I first met her. "We used to say we were engaged to be engaged."

"But Eric is deceased now?"

Her voice cracks, but she holds it together. "Yes, he was murdered."

I let her tell the story of Eric's partner, Michael Caruso, being murdered, and Eric going on the run as a fugitive. I have no doubt that the jury knows all about it, but I want to get it into the record again.

She wraps it up with, "I knew he was innocent. Now everyone knows it, but it's too late."

"While he was on the run, did he contact you?" I ask.

"Yes. He wanted me to bring his dog to him. Zoe." She goes on to explain that she had seen the picture of him that ran in Vince's paper, then picked up in papers nationally, which is how she and Eric both knew where Zoe was.

"Did he explain how Gerald Downey came to have Zoe?"

She nods. "Yes. He told me that he paid to have her stolen from you, so he could get her back." Her testimony skirts a fine line here, one we have gone over. Eric never mentioned Downey's name, so Stephanie does not either. But the strong implication is that Eric hired Downey, which is the actual truth.

I then take her through the tough part, the trip to Maine, and the discovery of Eric's and Healy's bodies. She handles it like a trouper, pausing to gather herself when she thinks she might break down.

To sum up, I ask her, "And you're sure the dog is Zoe?"

"No question about it."

"How is she doing?"

Stephanie breaks into a big smile. "She's doing wonderfully. We've been a big comfort to each other."

Dylan gets up to cross-examine. "Ms. Manning, besides what you may have heard from Mr. Carpenter, do you have any independent knowledge as to why Gerald Downey was murdered?"

"No."

"Do you have any independent knowledge as to who his killer was?"

"No."

"Do you have any independent knowledge as to why Eric Brantley was murdered?"

She hesitates. "No."

"Do you have any independent knowledge as to who his killer was?"

"No."

"But you have his dog."

"Yes."

"That's nice," he says, thereby effectively dismissing her testimony as unimportant. "No further questions."

My next witness is Dan Hendricks, the bartender working the night Tommy threatened to slit Gerald Downey's throat. He testified in Dylan's case, and I had a chance to cross-examine him, but I've called him back because I want to get him to talk about Downey's dubious associates.

Dylan objects to my questions, claiming they aren't relevant, but Klingman consistently overrules him. "That issue has been decided," Klingman finally says, sternly enough that I don't think Dylan will raise it again.

Hendricks doesn't know anything about the diamond smuggling, but he does know quite a few convicted felons who Downey counted as friends.

"Were any of them in the bar the night in question?"

"I don't remember," he says. "Well, once Downey was threatened, he went into the back and made a phone call. Two of his friends came to throw Mr. Infante out. I do know they have both spent some time in prison."

He's referring to the two guys who were foolish enough to mess with Marcus, but that's not what has struck me about his testimony. It's something else, something I hadn't caught on to before.

I finish with my questions, and Dylan gives him a brief cross-examination, mainly to drive home the fact that Hendricks really knows nothing of substance when it comes to the case we are trying.

As he is leaving the stand, I ask him to wait for me in the gallery. Judge Klingman adjourns court for the day, so I pat Tommy on the shoulder and walk over to where Hendricks is waiting.

"What do you want?" he asks. "I've got things to do"

"This won't take long," I say. "When I was at the bar, I wasn't getting cell service. Is that unusual?"

"Nah. Service is terrible there. People complain all the time."

"You said that Downey went into the back to call his friends to come throw Tommy out. Does that mean he would have used the landline in the office?"

"Yeah. My boss doesn't want it to be a habit, but if it was important, then sure."

"When he went into the back to make the call, how long was he gone?"

"I don't know; I wasn't timing him."

"Try and remember," I say.

He thinks for a while, and then says, "You know, I think it took a while. I remember wondering if he snuck out the back."

"What is the landline number at the bar?" I ask, and he tells me.

"You can go now," I say.

"Am I done talking to you?" he asks. "I mean, for good?"

"Now you've gone and hurt my feelings."

Before I head home, I call Sam and ask him to check out the bar phone number on the night that Downey called his friends.

I want to see who else he might have called.

The two boats had left port in northeastern Canada. The trip to Ashby would take about thirty hours, but there was no desire to get there that fast. Sitting off the coast of Maine could draw unwanted attention from the Coast Guard, and that was something they could not afford.

The larger of the two boats, almost eighty feet from stem to stern, was the important one. It was filled with weaponry, everything from laser-guided, shoulder-fired missiles, to grenade launchers, to mines, to assault rifles. The value of the cargo was close to 120 million dollars.

The second ship was much smaller, and carried no cargo at all. Its sole function was to carry off the crew of the first ship, after it had been turned over to the people who had purchased it. That rendezvous was a number of days away, after confirmation of payment received.

Once that was accomplished, the first ship would set sail and dock in Ashby.

And nothing after that would ever be the same.

Sam comes through again. Not only does he have the answer for me before I have to head for court this morning, but he has the answer I was looking for. Downey did in fact call the two goons to throw Tommy out of the bar, but he also called the same number that Professor Charles Horowitz had called.

Alan Divac's private line at his company.

When I arrive at court, I call Laurie, and ask her to get Marcus to come down to the courthouse as soon as possible.

As I do every morning, I spend a little time with Tommy in the anteroom, so he can ask me what his chances are, and I can evade the question by telling him I have no idea, or that it's too early to tell. Sometimes I throw in some nonsense about how unpredictable juries can be.

The net effect is that he understands we're in trouble, so I probably should just say that in the first place. I need to work on that.

Marcus appears within ten minutes of my call to Laurie; Marcus is simply always around when I need him. Sometimes I think there is more than one Marcus, though the concept is a frightening one.

He takes a seat in the still-empty gallery, not saying anything but knowing that I will notice him. Marcus is definitely someone you notice, whether surrounded by empty chairs, or in the middle of sixty thousand screaming fans at Yankee Stadium.

"Thanks for coming, Marcus," I say, a brilliant conversational opening gambit that does not draw any response at all. "My first witness today is a guy named Paul Turner. He's the key witness in a federal smuggling case, so he's being protected by marshals. They've got him holed up in a hotel, but he told me he doesn't want the protection, and is going to get away from them."

I pause for Marcus to comment, or nod, or blink, or do anything to show me that he's awake. He doesn't so I continue.

"There's a chance that he might try to get away from them today. If he does so before he testifies, please bring him right back. If it's after he testifies, which is what I suspect will happen, please follow him."

Again I pause, and again there is absolutely no response from Marcus.

So I go on. "I want to know where he is. It will give me leverage with the customs guys. That's pretty much it. Any questions?"

Nothing from Marcus.

"Great," I say. "I always enjoy our little chats."

The gallery starts to fill up, and of course the seats around Marcus are the last to be taken. A couple of minutes later I look over and Marcus is gone, though I have total confidence he understood what I asked him and will do it flawlessly.

Paul Turner comes in just before court is ready to begin, accompanied by two agents. He greets me with a handshake and a smile, and doesn't seem at all put off by being called to testify.

It is consistent with Hike having told me that Turner accepted the subpoena in a similar fashion.

"Are you all set?" I ask.

"I won't know that until I hear what you're going to ask me."

His comment fits in with my concern about having been unable to go over his testimony with him. "We're just having a conversation," I say. "Telling the truth. At least nobody can say you were coached."

He smiles. "My federal friends are worried about this. They're afraid I'll screw up their case."

"If you do, it means they didn't have a case in the first place."

Some witnesses are more important than others, and some are absolutely crucial. Paul Turner fits into the second category for me. He's the first and best witness I have to tie Gerald Downey into the diamond smuggling ring. So far I have been able to show that Downey hung around with some unsavory people. This is my chance to show that some of those people were killers.

"Mr. Turner, where have you been living these last couple of weeks?" I ask.

"In a hotel; I'd rather not say where."

"Why is that?"

"I'm being protected by the FBI, because I am a witness in a case the federal government is prosecuting," he says.

"What kind of case?"

"It involves diamond smuggling, and murder."

"And the FBI feels your life might be in danger, perhaps from those you are testifying against?"

"That's exactly right," he says.

"Are you frightened?"

He nods. "Let's say I'm concerned. I'm not used to knowing

that there are people who would prefer I were dead, and who are willing and able to make that happen."

I've opened in this manner both to demonstrate that there are dangerous people involved, but also to emphasize Turner's being an important federal witness. If the Feds trust him enough to base their case on him, then my feeling is the jury will trust him as well.

"Did you ever meet Gerald Downey?" I ask.

"I did not."

"Ever heard of him before he was murdered?"

He nods. "Yes. A number of times."

"How did you come to hear of him?"

"He was involved in a diamond smuggling operation run by my boss at the time, Alan Divac."

"What was Mr. Downey's role, if you know?"

"He was a low-level operative, not a significant strategist. His importance came in a particular contact he had," Turner says.

"Who would that be?"

"He knew a customs official at Port Newark who looked the other way when the illegal diamonds came into the country. His name was Gino Parelli."

"Do you see Mr. Parelli in the courtroom today?" I ask.

"No, he was murdered himself not long ago."

"Are you aware of anything that Mr. Downey did to anger his bosses in the smuggling operation?" I ask.

Turner nods. "Yes. He became involved with Eric Brantley, who was setting himself up as a competitor to Alan Divac."

"And Mr. Divac is a man who does not take kindly to competition and competitors?" I ask.

"That would be the understatement of the year."

"Where is Mr. Divac now?'

"In jail, awaiting trial," Turner says.

Dylan's first question on cross-examination is, "Mr. Turner, do you have any evidence that anyone other than the defendant murdered Mr. Downey?"

"No," Turner says. "Nor do I have any evidence that the defendant did it."

"I've got an idea," says Dylan. "Why don't you answer only the questions that I ask you, and then we can move this along. Okay?"

"Fine."

"Did you ever hear anyone threaten Mr. Downey?"

"No."

"Ever hear anyone say they were going to slit his throat?"

"No."

"Now you say that Mr. Downey was in a smuggling partnership with Eric Brantley?" Dylan asks.

"I didn't describe it as a partnership. I said he was involved with him."

"Did you ever meet Mr. Brantley?"

"No," Turner says.

"Ever see him with Mr. Downey?"

"No."

"Ever hear them discuss their partnership? Pardon me, their 'involvement'?"

"No."

"Is there anything that you've testified to today that you didn't hear secondhand?"

"I saw or heard almost all of Mr. Divac's dealings."

"And yet you never heard him order the murder of Mr. Downey?" Dylan asks.

"No, I did not."

"Thank you. No further questions."

I think Turner was an effective witness, and an intelligent, fair-minded juror should at least entertain the notion that Downey died as a result of what his diamond smuggling bosses considered his betrayal.

On the other hand, an intelligent fair-minded juror would have trouble getting past the fact that Tommy threatened to slit Downey's throat, just before he got his throat slit . . . by a knife buried in Tommy's backyard.

Turner leaves the stand and comes over and sits down near the defense table. When Judge Klingman adjourns the court session, Turner comes over and says, "Is there a room back there that I can wait in for a while? There are media people out front, and I want to avoid them."

"Sure," I say. "Follow me." I lead him to an anteroom in the back, the one where I meet with clients. "I'm sure you can stay in here until the media clear out."

He smiles. "Thanks. I'm not a big fan of crowds these days."

"I can understand it."

I leave him in the room. I have no doubt that he couldn't care less about the media, and instead is going to go out the back way to get away from his government protectors.

I just hope Marcus is following him.

Thirty-one strangers, entering this area of Maine, are an unusual occurrence, to say the least. That is why they separated into twos and threes, and most of them did not quite go all the way to Ashby. They were being extra careful, as the risk was not great. No one was going to see a few strangers and call in the Marines, yet that's pretty much what it would take to derail their operation.

The plan had been set in stone for a very long time. Four men of their group would go out in a twenty-five-foot motorboat which had already been rented. They would meet the boat carrying the arms, and board it.

The crew of that boat would leave in the second boat they had brought with them, and the four men would bring their cargo to shore. As they were doing it, the remaining twenty-seven members of their group would enter Ashby.

Once the arms reached shore, in a secluded area, most of the men would be there to help unload the arms and make them operable. Then, in rapid succession, they would blow up both the bridge separating Ashby from the mainland, the small police department, and the town hall.

Their force would be overwhelming, and most of the towns-people who did not go into hiding would be rounded up as hostages. Anyone who resisted would be killed.

The insurgents would declare the town to be in their control, and negotiations with the American government would begin. Those negotiations would go nowhere, and eventually force would be used to recapture the island.

During the course of that operation, every one of the insurgents and every inhabitant of the city would die.

In death there would be victory.

W here the hell is Paul Turner?" asks Agent Hernandez. He was waiting for me in my office when I got back from court, along with a guy he introduced as Agent Phil Brooks of the FBI. Brooks has so far not said a word, but his facial expression is such that I've got a feeling I'm not going to like whatever he has to say, whenever he says it.

"How the hell should I know?" is my response. "Why don't you ask the agents who are protecting him?"

"They said he went with you into a room in the back of the courtroom, and they never saw him again."

"They sound like really good protectors. I have no idea where he is. He said he wanted somewhere to sit until the media people cleared out, so I showed him where he could sit." So far everything I've said is true, including not knowing where he is. I haven't heard a thing from Marcus yet.

"Don't screw around with us, Carpenter. This is too important."

"I'm telling you the truth," I say. "Whether or not you believe me is not something that's going to keep me up nights. And by the way, why would I want to hide Paul Turner from you?"

Hernandez looks at Brooks, in a gesture that seems like he is turning me over to him. Brooks nods and speaks for the first time.

"Carpenter, you may be telling the truth and have no idea where Turner is. But if you do know, and you don't tell us, you will go away for a long time; I will see to that. Are you familiar with the phrase, 'You're going down hard'?"

"Sure, I've heard it; that's an easy one," I say. "I love word games. My turn, my turn. Are you familiar with the phrase, 'Get the hell out of my office'?"

Agent Brooks looks like he is going to kill me, but opts against it, probably because it would involve too much paperwork. Instead he gives me his card, threatens me again, and leaves.

He has certainly left me with a lot to think about, and I head home to do it.

I have a quick dinner with Laurie and Ricky, then retreat to the den to figure out my next steps in a number of areas. Just as I'm settling in, the phone rings and Laurie gets it. A couple of minutes later, she comes into the den.

"That was Marcus," she says. "Turner is in a house in Alpine; he appears to be alone. I have the address."

"Good."

"Should Marcus keep on him?"

"Absolutely."

One thing I am thankful for, and that is the fact that today is Friday. I have big decisions to make regarding our case; in fact, it's the biggest decision of all. I have to decide whether or not Tommy Infante will testify in his own defense.

He wants to; he's said so on at least three occasions, and I certainly don't blame him. If I were facing these charges, and I were innocent, I'd want to get in the jurors' faces and scream it at them. The idea of possibly being convicted without speaking out in his own defense is an awful one to him.

But Tommy has also made it clear that I am in charge, and that he will go along with whatever decision I make. The temptation to let him testify is great, but the potential downside is enormous.

Under cross-examination, or maybe on direct, Tommy would have to explain why he threatened Downey in that bar. He couldn't take refuge in the nonpayment of his share of the jewelry robbery, because there was no such robbery. Dylan would nail him on it, and Tommy would have perjured himself.

To tell the truth, that Healy paid him to do it, is even worse. It would align Tommy with the diamond smugglers, and make him one of their group. Our entire case has been based on getting the jurors to believe that the killers came from that ring; if Tommy admits to being a part of their operation, in whatever capacity, it turns our case on its head.

Even though court does not reconvene until Monday, I have to make the decision quickly. If Tommy is going to testify, I'll need to spend most of the weekend with him, going over his testimony. If not, then I'll need to get my closing statement ready.

It's hard for me to focus on the issue, because my mind, which has a mind of its own, wants to ponder the visit from Agents Hernandez and Brooks today after court.

After Laurie puts Ricky to bed, I ask her to come in so we can talk about it. I describe the conversation, and ask her what she makes of it.

"The interesting thing to me is that the FBI now seems to be in charge," she says.

I nod. "I was thinking the same thing. It's a customs case that gets destroyed if Turner doesn't return to testify against Divac. But the FBI guy, Brooks, seemed more anxious than Hernandez."

"Which means that more than the customs case is at stake," she says.

"They're worried about something way bigger than the case; I just don't know what it is. But it fits in with Cindy having told me that lives are at stake."

"Are you going to tell them where Turner is?"

"I might, if I could figure out why having Turner in their protection saves any lives other than his. Until then, I think I'll hang on to that hole card."

"Is that a poker phrase?" she asks. "I didn't know you play poker."

"There's a lot you don't know about me, babe. You're just scratching the surface."

"Maybe I should stop scratching."

The defense rests," I say, when Judge Klingman asks if we have any more witnesses.

Dylan looks surprised; he probably spent the entire weekend
preparing to cross-examine Tommy. The courteous thing would
have been to tell him my plans, but since it was Dylan, I never
considered doing so.

But to his credit, he is always prepared, and when Judge
Klingman asks if he is ready to deliver his closing statement, he
doesn't hesitate.

"Ladies and gentlemen, first of all I want to thank you for
your service. It is not easy for you to do what you have done here,
but it is necessary for the preservation of our justice system, and
indeed our democracy, and no one can say you have not come
through.

"When we first convened here, I told you that this was basically a straightforward case, and that is just as true today.
Mr. Carpenter has regaled you with stories about the bad people
Mr. Downey associated with, but has not offered the slightest
shred of evidence that any of them took Mr. Downey's life.

"Sometimes, actually quite frequently, we find that murder
victims have associated with less than completely honorable

people. But the only dishonorable person you need to concern yourself with is the one who committed the murder, and that is Thomas Infante.

"When Judge Klingman discussed your responsibilities, he certainly did not instruct you to check your common sense at the door. And if you follow that common sense, then here is all you need to know:

"In a fit of rage, Thomas Infante told Gerald Downey he was going to kill him. He told him how he was going to kill him. He told him why he was going to kill him.

"And that's exactly what he did.

"It's rare that a killer, from his own mouth, provides us with the motive and the method. But Mr. Infante went a step further: he provided us with the murder weapon, by burying it in his backyard.

"Don't make this more complicated than it is. Don't let all this talk about international smuggling rings, and sinister cloak-and-dagger figures, distract you from what remains a very simple case.

"Thomas Infante brutally murdered Gerald Downey, and you must hold him responsible for his actions. Simple as that."

Dylan has done a very effective job of presenting his case; right now if I was on the jury I'd probably vote to convict. And if I don't effectively blunt his message, that is exactly what these jurors are going to do.

"Gerald Downey did not deserve to die, and he certainly did not deserve to die the way he did" is how I start. "I think everyone in this courtroom can agree on that. I know you must want to punish someone for it, and so do I. It's a natural reaction.

"But that is not your job. Your job is to determine whether or not Thomas Infante is the one who should be punished. And if you say he is, and you're wrong, then it only makes things worse, much worse.

"If you have a reasonable doubt as to Thomas Infante's guilt, then you have to trust the system. You have to trust that the real killer will be found, and that citizens just like you will make the correct judgment about that person. That's all you can do; it's all anyone asks you to do.

"You've been bombarded with facts; I don't envy you having to sort through them. I'd like to focus on one area right now, if I may. You've heard witnesses, people in a position to know, tell you that Gerald Downey was involved in a diamond smuggling ring.

"Paul Turner, the lead witness in a federal prosecution of the leader of that ring, laid it out for you chapter and verse. He told you Downey's role in the operation, in detail.

"But even more importantly, he described the fate of other members of that ring, and what he said wasn't opinion, it was fact. Eric Brantley was killed . . . that's a fact. Michael Caruso was killed . . . that's a fact. Professor Charles Horowitz was killed . . . that's a fact. Gino Parelli was killed . . . that's a fact. And the list goes on.

"No one is claiming, not Mr. Campbell, not the FBI, no one, that Thomas Infante killed any of those people. He has the best alibi one could ever have; he was in jail awaiting trial.

But somebody murdered them, and Mr. Turner has told you that they died as a result of their smuggling activities. The same smuggling activities that Gerald Downey was a part of."

I stop for a moment, as a realization sinks in. It is strange how the mind works, and I would imagine that mine is stranger than most. Things hit me at the weirdest times; I just can't control it. This is certainly not the most opportune time, when I'm in the middle of addressing the jury, and it leaves me so stunned that I lose my train of thought.

It is not easy, but I recover and continue. "With so many people suffering the same fate at the hands of the same people, can you actually say that Gerald Downey did not do so as well? Can you say that, beyond a reasonable doubt? I would submit that you cannot.

"Thomas Infante is guilty: he is guilty of acting stupidly, and setting himself up as a patsy. Threatening Gerald Downey in the way he did made him a perfect candidate to be set up, and that is what happened.

"No, Gerald Downey did not deserve to die. And Thomas Infante does not deserve to go to prison. It is too late to right that first wrong, but not the second. That is in your hands. Thank you."

I sit down next to Tommy, who whispers "thank you" to me. I think I did pretty well, but right now it's one of the furthest things from my mind. All I want is for Judge Klingman to read his charge to the jury and let me get to a telephone.

It takes almost forty-five minutes for court to be finally adjourned, and the jury sent off to begin their deliberations. It's among the forty-five longest minutes I can ever remember.

I go back to the anteroom, the same one I left Paul Turner in that day. I'm alone, so I take out my cell phone and dial FBI Agent Brooks, reading his phone number off the card he gave me.

He answers the phone on the third ring, and I say, "Agent Brooks, this is Andy Carpenter."

"I'm listening," he says.

"Good, because I'm talking, and you are a son of a bitch."

"That's what you called to tell me?"

"That's part of it," I say. "The other part is this: from this point on, from this very moment, we are playing by my rules."

The house in Alpine where Paul Turner is staying is in a heavily wooded area. It's a log-cabin style, but not the kind Abe Lincoln was born in. It's the kind that Abe Lincoln would have been born in if his father had owned a hedge fund.

There's a long dirt road driveway through the trees, and Marcus meets me at the end of it. He's on foot; I have no idea where his car is. If he were wearing a cape, I would assume he had flown in.

As we are walking toward the house, I tell Marcus what I hope to accomplish in my conversation with Turner. The trees have more of a reaction than Marcus does, but I know he's heard me.

The house itself is very large and obviously very expensive. I can see partway into the area behind the house; there is a large pool and tennis court. Turner has not been suffering in his time here.

Strangely, there is no doorbell, so I knock loudly on the heavy wooden front door. Within thirty seconds, I see movement at a front window; Turner is peering out to see who his visitor is. He must be okay with the fact that it's me, because a few seconds later, he opens the door.

He doesn't seem stressed, and smiles when he asks, "What the hell are you doing here?"

"We were in the neighborhood. Can we come in?"

"Of course."

I introduce Marcus to Turner, and I'm sure he has no idea what to make of him.

"Thanks for helping me get out of that courtroom," Turner says. "But how did you find out I was here?"

"I had you followed."

"Why?"

"So I could bring you back if I had to. The Feds are pressuring me to do that."

He loses the smile and casual tone. "There is no way I'm going back. Neither you, nor your friend here, can make me do that. I'm much safer here."

"I figured that would be your reaction," I say, trying to conceal my nervousness. "So I've come up with a handy alternative."

"Which is?" he asks.

"Ten million dollars in diamonds. Real ones. Not Brantley's fakes."

He almost does a double take, but then actually laughs. This is one unworried guy. "You've got more chance of taking me back." Then, "How did you figure it out?"

I shrug. "Actually, I'm embarrassed it took me so long. I should have seen it sooner; you saw an opportunity to push Divac out and set yourself up for one huge, final score."

"What gave it away?" he asks.

"Well, for one thing, Parelli was killed not long after I told you I had identified him to the customs people. I didn't mention his name, but that didn't matter, because you already knew who he was. And in that same conversation, you told me you knew almost nothing about my case."

"So?"

"So Divac knew all about it when we met, and he as much as said that you had done the research for him. You lied to me, and people always lie for a reason."

"Not bad," Turner says. "Go on."

"When Downey called on Divac's private line from the bar, it was late. Bosses tend to go home early, but as Divac's right-hand man, you would have had access to his private line. But most importantly, you never told the Feds or me that Brantley wasn't bringing in diamonds, he was creating them. There was no way you couldn't have known that."

"I'm impressed," he says. "Divac never even figured that out."

"He didn't know Brantley's diamonds were fake?"

He laughs. "No way. Divac loves diamonds . . . actually, literally loves those stupid little rocks. He would never go for that."

"Did Healy kill Gerry Downey?"

"He did, in an effort to find Brantley. Healy lost his ability to bring in diamonds, so he needed Brantley. And Divac was in the dark about all of it."

"So that's how you knew you could set him up?"

This time there is no laughing. "I took his shit for years, and never saw any real money. He didn't think I knew what was going on, so I waited for the right opportunity, and made my move. I'm going to make more money on one deal than you could make in a lifetime chasing ambulances."

"Where are the arms going?" I ask.

"What the hell is the difference? You won't be around to read about it."

"Then humor me."

Turner thinks about it for a moment before responding. "Let's just say that the invasion of Ashby, Maine, will be the most famous since Normandy. These lunatics are willing to die for—"

"Shut up."

Neither Turner, Marcus, nor I said that, so I've got a hunch there is someone else in the room. A look to the side confirms that. It's a very large man, at least six-four, with an intense face and chiseled body. But that's not the worst part. The worst part is that he's holding a gun.

"Alek," I say. "Supplier of arms, and international asshole."

He doesn't say anything to me; instead he talks to Turner. "You talk too much."

If Turner is intimidated by Alek, he hides it well. "There is no harm; they're not leaving here alive."

Alek moves to maybe ten or twelve feet in front of us, still pointing the gun. He looks most intently at Marcus, sizing him up. "I think I would like to take you apart with my bare hands."

"You should try it," I say, my heart pounding. "I'll hold your gun."

Once again I'm ignored, and Alek says to Turner, "Check them for weapons."

Turner walks over and frisks us. It's a perfunctory effort, but he does find a small pistol that Marcus carries in his pocket.

"Throw it over there," Alek says, and Turner does so. Turner then starts walking back toward Alek, but Alek stops him by pointing the gun at him. "You stand with them."

"What are you doing?" Turner asks, for the first time showing a major crack in his cool façade. My sense is that they have been equals, Turner selling the diamonds and supplying the money, and Alek selling the arms. That equality seems to have ended rather quickly.

"When all those Americans die, they will come after us with all they have. You are just another weak link that I am removing."

"No," Turner says, as Alek points the gun again. Turner is

standing just a couple feet in front of us, when all of a sudden he isn't there anymore. I haven't heard a gunshot, and it takes me an instant to realize what has actually happened, and is happening.

Marcus has moved forward and clamped his hands onto Turner's sides, lifting him about six inches off the ground. He rushes toward Alek, holding Turner in front of him as if he were a child's toy, but actually using him as a shield.

Alek fires the gun, I think twice, and I see Turner shake from the impact, as blood flies. Marcus and his shield have by now reached Alek, and he heaves Turner's body at him, sending them both to the floor, with Turner on top.

From a prone position, Alek tries to raise his gun, but Marcus is too fast: he kicks it out of his hand. Alek starts to get to his feet, but Marcus clubs him on the left side of his head with his right hand, elbow, and forearm, hitting Alek with a sickeningly beautiful thud.

Alek's head and body are knocked to the side, but the momentum is stopped by a similar blow from Marcus's left arm, coming up and crushing the left side of Alek's face. It actually lifts him off the ground in the opposite direction. It's as if Marcus has used Alek's head as a pinball.

I look down at Alek's now lifeless body. "How'd that 'bare hands' thing work out for you?" I ask, but he doesn't answer.

Suddenly the room looks like an FBI convention, as agents flood into the house, guns drawn, with Brooks in the lead.

"What the hell took you so long?" I ask.

Brooks shrugs. "We needed to make sure we got the information we needed. Worked out pretty well." Then he looks down at Alek's smashed head. "Holy shit," he says.

Brooks looks over at Marcus, logically assuming that I wasn't the one who smashed Alek's head. "You okay?" Brooks asks, and then I see that Marcus has a bullet wound in his shoulder. It must have passed through Turner's body.

"Yuh," Marcus says. Apparently when he gets shot he gets talkative.

"Get him looked at," Brooks says.

One of the agents leads Marcus out, and I say to Brooks, "I upheld my end of the bargain."

He nods. "Yes you did."

The United States has 12,383 miles of coast-line. It is clearly too long to be patrolled on an ongoing basis, but that has not been a particular problem, since no foreign entity has ever tried to invade. And there are very few military planners who would expect the first attack to be in the area of Ashby, Maine.

When Agent Brooks put in the call, he had no way of knowing that five minutes earlier, the transfer was made at sea, and the invaders had taken over the boat loaded with the deadly armaments. They were about to head for Ashby, a trip that would take ninety minutes.

The military response was threefold. Two Coast Guard Cutters, on patrol from Sector Northern New England headquarters, were immediately dispatched to the area. Two hundred and fifty army reservists were ordered flown in from Fort Drum in upstate New York, and the Maine State Police deployed in full force as well. Local police units were put on alert, but not given an immediate assignment.

Most importantly, because speed was of the essence, air assets were brought in from Otis Air National Guard Base on Cape

Cod and Langley Air Force Base in Virginia. A-10 attack airplanes were assigned the task.

The planes were the first to arrive, buzzing low over the ship and attempting, without success, to establish radio contact. Fortunately, in this situation, nonverbal communication was all that was necessary to convey to the invaders the very clear message: turn around or be destroyed.

It was immediately apparent to the men on the ship that they had no decent options. They could stop, and wait for American vessels to arrive, board, and take them into custody. Or they could continue on to Ashby, almost guaranteeing that either the airplanes or those ships would blow them out of the water.

Death did not scare them; they had been prepared for that. But failure was simply unacceptable.

So they continued on, and the planes did not attack. Two Coast Guard vessels arrived, and through loudspeakers ordered the ship to stop and be boarded. They disregarded the instructions and continued on.

The ship was about forty minutes from the coast of Maine when the order came, and the A-10's fired three missiles. One would have been more than sufficient, and what had been a ship was instantly transformed into human and metal debris.

It was left to the soldiers, and state police, to find and arrest the invaders who had already entered Ashby, or were preparing to do so. This was done quickly; the only two people who resisted were killed.

Everything was done with such efficiency that many of the residents of Ashby only learned of their close call through the media.

It is pretty close to a perfect moment. At my insistence, the announcement that the charges against Tommy Infante have been dismissed is being done at a press conference. I know it will get more attention than a simple press release, and Tommy deserves that.

I also had insisted that Dylan make the announcement. I did this for no reason other than I knew it would be something that he would despise doing, which would in turn make it more enjoyable for me. And I have to admit I am relishing his obvious discomfort.

Dylan says that he can't give out too much information, for security reasons, but that the dismissal does not simply mean that the charges could not be proven. It means that Thomas Infante is innocent, that he had been wrongly accused.

Agent Hernandez has been good enough to show up for this press conference, and he had some interesting things to tell me before it started. Now that Turner has been exposed, Divac has been talking, as part of a plea bargain. Healy was working for him, but he apparently panicked when he lost his contacts to bring in diamonds. He knew Divac wouldn't go for Brantley's fakes, so he set out to get them on his own. Divac claims to have been in the dark about all of this, and Hernandez believes him.

Divac didn't realize that Turner knew about his illegal smuggling activities, but Turner saw everything, and moved in when he saw the opportunity.

Turner set Divac up, and then he and Alek combined forces to take over the operation. The ironic thing was that neither cared at all about the events that were to take place in Ashby; they were just in it for the money.

To make today's event that much sweeter, it turns out that the jury's initial vote was nine-three to convict. Dylan could have won.

Heh, heh.

Tommy and I happily watch Dylan's discomfort from behind the podium, on the stage. As he finishes and exits, we are asked to take questions, but we decline to do so. Tommy simply walks to the microphone and says, "It's a huge relief to me that justice and Andy Carpenter prevailed."

What a nice speech.

W e have our traditional victory party at Charlie's, even though it wasn't a traditional victory. Tommy is of course here, as is Stephanie Manning. Our whole team is present: Willie and Sondra, Laurie, Hike, Edna, Sam, Hilda and Eli Mandlebaum, Morris Fishman, and Leon Goldberg. Marcus is here also, bearing no apparent ill effects of a gunshot wound. Marcus is a tad unusual.

Sam said that Hilda, Eli, Morris, and Leon are usually in bed by eight, so in deference to them we start the party at six o'clock. Vince and Pete are here as well, and Vince complains about the early start. "What the hell is this, the breakfast club?"

"The beer and food are on me, Vince."

"On the other hand, time is not important. In China it's tomorrow already, right? Or yesterday?" Vince says. "Anyway, I'm a morning person."

Tommy spends most of the night thanking everyone, and near the end of the night, meaning almost eight o'clock, he corners me. "How did you get them to clear me?"

"The Feds knew much more than they let on," I say. "Hernandez lied to me when he said Turner was clean; they knew he was dirty and they were hoping he'd run. They just screwed up;

they wanted to be the ones to follow him. They knew something big was going to happen on American soil, but they didn't know it was going to be Ashby. They needed to know where the arms were going, so I struck a deal with them."

"Did they know I didn't kill Downey?"

"I believe they did, but I'm not positive. But they were certainly fine with pressuring the DA to dismiss the charges. I think the order came down from the office of the goddamn attorney general."

"If they didn't make the deal, would you have given them Turner?"

I think about it for a few moments; it hadn't been a decision that I had made. "I would have, yes. People were going to die. But I would have gone public with everything and made them look stupid."

"Man, I lucked out when you showed up," he says. "And all because of that dog."

"How's your daughter?" I ask.

"I talked to Jenny and her mother a few minutes ago. I think she's going to be okay, but it's day to day."

Stephanie comes over with a cell phone full of pictures of Zoe. "Zoe's doing great," she says.

"What about you?" I ask.

"Getting there, Andy. I'm getting there."

"I'm glad to hear that, and I'm here if you need me."

"Eric wasn't a bad person, Andy. He just made a mistake."

"I'm sorry it ended that way," I say.

Hilda has made some of her rugelach for the party, and I think Vince would eat four hundred of them if he could. He keeps coming over and saying, "Have you tasted these? Have you tasted these?"

Hilda and Eli are having a great time; they are obviously

party animals. I think they'd stay and close the place, as long as the place closed at eight-thirty.

Laurie and I have to get home; our sitter can only stay until eight o'clock.

And tomorrow is a big day.

Opening day is always special. I remember going to opening day at Yankee Stadium with my father when I was no more than eight years old. The green grass was stunning in its beauty, and even though we were sitting fairly far down the left field foul line, I felt like I was on the field with the players. I brought my scorebook, and dutifully recorded every play.

Today's experience is somewhat different. We're on the Little League field at Eastside Park, for an arranged game between Ricky's School Number 20 team, and the hated rivals from School Number 26. It's Ricky's first semi-official game, and he's all excited, as are Laurie and I.

We sit in the stands with about forty other parents, and the first thing I notice is that there is no scoreboard. I point this out to Laurie, and she says, "Didn't I mention that? They're not going to keep score. They want to emphasize the fun aspect, not the competition."

"Not going to keep score? How do you know who wins?"

"Nobody wins," she says. "And nobody loses. That's the point."

This is bizarre. "So who gets mocked afterward?" I ask.

"Andy—"

"I'll keep the score myself."

"You do that," she says.

A few minutes before the game starts, Ricky comes over to us, all excited. "I'm playing shortstop! That's good, right?"

Finally, talent has been recognized. "That's great, Rick!" both Laurie and I say, simultaneously.

The game begins, and the first batter for the other team hits a dribbler to third, and winds up on second base. The next batter hits a slow ground ball to Ricky's right. He smoothly ambles over, looking like Derek Jeter on his best day. But instead of fielding the ball with his glove, he accidentally kicks it with his right foot.

The ball heads straight for the third base bag, and the third baseman grabs it and tags out the runner trying to advance from second.

It was a perfect kick by Ricky.

Maybe soccer is his thing.